ALL IN YOUR HEAD

Gaby Knight

ALL IN YOUR HEAD
Copyright © 2025 by Gaby Knight

Contact: gknightauthor@gmail.com

Cover Design: Julia Horobets

Editor: Sarah Waterman

ISBN: 979-8-9923934-2-2 (paperback) 979-8-9923934-3-9 (hardcover)

To my 11-year-old self and to all middle school girls with racing hearts and intrusive thoughts.
It's okay. You're okay. You will be okay.

Prologue

Clink. A coffee bean hits the glass, then falls softly to the ground.

Clink. A second coffee bean hits the window. He waits for her to respond. Nothing yet.

Clink. He's ready to go as he feels a single raindrop hit his head. He looks up to the menacing sky growing darker by the minute. He hadn't dressed for rain, thinking he'd be inside already.

Clink. Is she ignoring him? He thought her husband was gone.

Clink. Doesn't matter, anyways. Tonight is the night. They've been planning this forever.

Creak. The door opens as he was readying another coffee bean. She stands there, radiant as ever. It looks like she's been cooking with her stained handmade apron hanging around her neck. He takes a step in and clears his throat, ready to speak his truth. The rain is now pouring down hard, splattering against the window. *Perfect timing,* he thinks. It's now or never.

Chapter One

It's so over. Just give up. There's no way you know this. There's no way you can do this. It's over, it's over, it's over. Might as well flunk out, run away with a seventh grade education and inevitably become a drifter for the rest of your life. Your parents won't recognize you as a shriveled, dirty person, walking around with the pigeons in the city. It's so over.

Cass' heart was thumping as she stared at the paper with her pre-algebra test printed on it. Solving for X shouldn't be hard, but why are fractions involved?

Cass took a deep breath as she looked up from her test and observed the classroom around her.

Lenore Hurley, her best friend sitting diagonally in front of her, was already done and now reading her worn out copy of *The Hound of Baskervilles*. Cass sighed with envy as she glanced back at her exam and did her best to finish. She solved the last problem as the bell rang and handed it in to her teacher.

Lenore waited for her at the door before they started toward their next class. Cass put her hand to her forehead.

"That was so hard," she murmured.

"Not really," Lenore replied. "I got through it okay. How do you think you did?"

"I don't want to talk about it," Cass started. "But I started getting those thoughts again. And my heart was pounding."

"Whoa," Lenore said, trying to be discreet. "What was your pre-cog telling you?"

"Not sure," Cass said. "I don't think I need to give up trying on my test or anything. I don't plan on running away with a seventh-grade education."

"What about your cross-country meet?" Lenore suggested. "You are rematching state champions again."

"Meh, I don't feel really nervous about that," Cass said. "I think I outpace a few of those girls, anyways."

Both turned down the hall to enter their English classroom.

"Maybe you're—" Lenore was cut off as a herd of sixth graders ran down the hall, no doubt trying to make it to class before the bell. One of them pushed Cass in the back and she tripped, dropping her small stack of books, and sending papers everywhere. Lenore bent over and helped Cass gather all of her things as the class bell rang.

Their elderly, lanky teacher Mrs. Leary stood in front of the door as the girls grabbed everything and got up. She was a known strict teacher, and Cass felt herself brace for the words she was going to use to cut them.

"Tardiness is always inexcusable," she started. "This time, though, it seems it wasn't caused by your own actions. Come in so we don't spoil everyone's learning time now, Miss Fairchild and Miss Hurley."

Cass and Lenore exchanged surprised looks before sitting in the front row. Cass' heart slowed and the negative thoughts dropped off as the pace of class slowly moved along. Maybe the herd of sixth graders was what her premonition was warning her about? They stopped her from getting to class on time, and she hadn't seen them coming. Cass considered this while trying to take notes.

Eventually, Mrs. Leary's droning stopped as the school bell let out for the day.

The next thing they knew, Cass and Lenore were at The Roast of Moon Town to celebrate the end of the school week. While Lenore's mom was busy wrangling her twins, Jennie and Jeanine, around the place, the girls were waiting impatiently at the counter for their sugary drinks.

"Well I guess that could be the reason for the premonition," Lenore said. "Hopefully the next time you get one, we've already made it to class. I thought Mrs. Leary was going to give us lunch detention."

"Yeah, I'd rather not get an elbow to the back going to her class ever again."

"One black coffee for Edward," a barista yelled out as he put the small cup of coffee on the counter.

"Excuse me, ladies," a geriatric man said gently as he tried to part between them. He quickly grabbed his coffee.

"Sorry, Mr. Benson," Cass said.

"Yeah, sorry," Lenore added.

"What was that?" He gingerly asked. "You children talk too fast."

"WE'RE SORRY FOR BEING IN THE WAY," Lenore said loudly.

"No need to shout, dear!" Mr. Benson said as he let out a little laugh. "I readjusted my hearing aid." Then he hurriedly made his way to his window seat for one. He sipped his drink as he looked out the window.

The girls soon got their smoothies and sat down at one of the couches as Lenore's mom chased the twins.

"Mr. Benson is so old," Cass said.

"I know," Lenore said. "He probably lives alone, that's why he can't comprehend our youthful voices."

"He's probably one of those introverts who brags about living in isolation because they can't go crazy."

"Yeah, and what if one time, kidnappers stole his family, and at first he missed them, but then he liked living in solitude!"

"Yeah, and the kidnappers eventually returned them, so now

he comes here every week to get a break from them!"

"Girls!" Cass and Lenore jumped in their seats before realizing Lenore's mom was behind them with the twins in her arms. "Don't make up stories about other people in public."

"Sorry," they both mumbled. They drank their smoothies and watched Lenore's little sisters bounce up and down while her mom grabbed her own drink. Ten minutes later, Mr. Benson got up from his perch and left the cafe as her mom sat back down.

"Hey mom, don't you think it's a little weird our neighbor Mr. Benson is only seen here in public and he never has anyone with him? He's always by himself and he doesn't try to talk to anyone."

"Lenore," her mom sighed. "Some people like living alone. He's independent! Just because he hasn't told you anything about himself doesn't mean his life is empty or lonely. You never know what's going on in someone's life until they reveal it to you."

"Sure, but that doesn't mean I can't entertain myself by making up stories about him," Lenore joked. Cass laughed as Mrs. Hurley realized Jeanine had gotten out of her spot and was running around tables.

Chapter Two

Cass got home around six that evening. The smell of spaghetti dinner wafted through the house. Her mom was making pasta for her cross-country meet the next morning.

"Hey, Cass!" her mom called from the stove. "How are you?"

Cass walked past her nine-year-old brother Tommy watching YouTube videos in the living room and into the kitchen.

"Hey, mom," she said as she kissed her baby sister Lucy, who was sitting in her high chair. Cass took a seat at the kitchen island next to the baby. "I'm okay, but I felt my heart racing during my math test."

Lucy started screaming then, so Cass picked her up and started bouncing her. Her mom's back was still turned to the stove.

"That's nice, honey," her mom said, mindlessly stirring the marinara sauce. Lucy's screaming had turned to gurgling noises, satisfied she was getting attention again.

"Yeah, and then a giant earthquake rocked the school into two, and the art room fell through the Earth. Lenore and I are the sole survivors, so I guess school is canceled forever," Cass said, rolling her eyes.

"Okay, honey," her mom nodded, still cooking. "Are you ready for tomorrow's meet? Your dad will take you since I have to provide snacks for Tommy's soccer game tomorrow."

"Okay," Cass held herself back from her mom's change of topic. She put Lucy back in her high chair and grabbed plates from the cabinets to set the dinner table.

Cass looked out the dining room window, hoping her dad would be home soon. She didn't see him much with him being a surgeon and all. He was saving lives and helping people at St. Dymphna Hospital, but she still wished she could see him during the week. At least she'd get time with him tomorrow.

Cass finished setting the table before her mom called them all to dinner.

✳✳✳

Her knees lightly bouncing, Cass looked around at everyone at the starting line the next day. She caught the stares of some of her competitors, also with slicked-backed ponytails and "eat my dust" written in sharpie on their arms. Something felt off. Her heart thumped in her chest. She turned and saw her teammate Katie Crombie looking green in the face.

"Hey Katie, are you okay?" Cass asked.

Katie nodded as she looked down.

Suddenly, the gun was shot and everyone took off running. Cass awkwardly started a side run before correcting her posture and running straight. She started passing and outpacing other girls, but as she ran through some thickets, she kept thinking about Katie. Maybe her precognition was telling her something about her teammate?

Cass dropped to a jog to look back for Katie. It took a few minutes, but she spotted her straggling in the back of a group. Katie stopped running suddenly, turning to a tree. Cass ran to her, holding her hair back as she threw up in some bushes. After a few minutes, Katie stopped hurling and wiped her mouth on her arm.

"Let me help you," Cass put her arm under Katie's shoulder and they slowly started walking.

After a few steps, Katie spoke up. "I think I got it," she croaked.

"Okay," Cass replied. The two started to jog slowly. For the rest of the race, they ran in silence.

"Thanks, Cass," Katie tried to find her words as the finish line came into view.

"You're welcome," Cass said. She paused for a second. "I had a strong feeling something like this was going to happen."

Chapter Three

Cass and Katie finished dead last at 51st and 52nd place, respectively. The girls' team placed fourth overall. Guilt started eating at Cass as she looked at her disappointed teammates, knowing she could have easily placed in the top ten.

"Before we go, let me name our team MVPs," Coach Webber said. "For the boys, Lucas Matthews. For girls, Cass Fairchild."

Cass snapped her head up to see Coach Webber smiling at her and Lucas. Lucas placed first for the boys and set a new personal record. Why was she named? Some of the girls around her rolled their eyes and murmured.

"It's not about who places the highest, but who shows true sportsmanship," Webber continued. "For taking care of one of our own, Cass is our most valuable player."

Unlike the others, Jada Lewis high-fived her and gave a "good job" before running off to her parents. Cass still felt pink in the face from the awkwardness as she walked toward her dad. He gave her a big hug and a smile before they got in his truck.

On their way to post-race Starbucks, her dad started asking more about her race.

"So, what made you stop for Katie? Weren't you ahead of

her?" He pulled into a parking spot.

"I was feeling kinda light, and my heart was beating—" Cass was cut off by her dads's phone ringing.

"Sorry, honey, let me check," he grabbed his phone, then answered it. They continued walking into the store. "Hey, Chris. No… No, the interns are supposed to be off today! Well tell them to go home and study if they want to learn so badly…"

He turned to Cass and gave her his credit card. "Hey, get me a small black coffee."

Cass sighed quietly before ordering the drinks while her dad stood by a window arguing with his coworker. Cass watched him from the counter for a few minutes, then heard their order get called. She grabbed the drink carrier in one hand and her slice of lemon pound cake in another and walked to him as he hung up.

"Hey, sweetie, I'm so sorry about that." Her dad started as he grabbed his drink. He grabbed the door to let her out and back to his car. "What were we talking about?"

"How I could tell Katie was sick. It was really just based on a feeling," Cass said as she sipped her orange smoothie.

"Hey, that's some pretty good intuition!" he said, encouragingly.

"Yeah, I suppose," Cass said coolly.

✳✳✳

Cass was never going to tell her family about her precog. If she told them, they might call her crazy, send her to an asylum, or let the government experiment on her. At least that's what she thought every time she thought of telling them. Her family loved her, but what if her premonitions jeopardized that?

After telling Lenore a year ago, her best friend vowed to keep her secret. Lenore was on the same thought wave as Cass. Plus, if Cass ever told anyone her secret and got taken away, she'd miss

Lenore.

Cass moved with her family to Moon Town the summer before she started middle school. Her dad had made a career move for St. Dymphna Hospital, and she reluctantly accepted it. Cass had been nervous to start at a new school, about fitting in and not wanting to change her personality. She liked the outdoors, reading, and still playing pretend. She wasn't worried about appearing cool or trendy.

Meeting Lenore Hurley in homeroom on the first day of school had been a godsend. She'd never met someone as silly and awesome as Lenore. Both learned elvish so they could send notes only the other could read. They explored the woods behind Lenore's house, and they buddy-read their favorite books.

They had fun pretending to both be Sherlock Holmes and making up stories and assumptions of strangers they saw in public. Sometimes they let it get wacky until a parent told them to stop being so loud.

Cass was blonde-haired and gray-eyed, the yin to Lenore's brown-haired and blue-eyed yang, the quiet to Lenore's loud, and the sweet to Lenore's salty. Both loved sports as well, which bonded them as their gangly heights matched at five foot three. Cass used her energy for cross-country, but ran into Lenore after her volleyball practice.

When Cass started feeling heart palpitations and racing thoughts during class last year, Lenore was the one person she could trust. Lenore didn't judge her or make fun of her. In fact, she seemed to embrace it. She was the one who pointed out it could be precognition.

They became convinced Cass had precognition after she predicted her mom was having a baby early. The two girls were hanging out when her heart started racing out of nowhere. Five minutes later, Lenore's mom got the call that Mrs. Fairchild went into labor two weeks early with Lucy. Cass had felt a connection to her baby sister ever since holding her the first time.

Another time, Cass and Lenore were out exploring the woods

when the former started getting feelings of dread. As soon as they started heading back to Lenore's house, they saw a coyote in her backyard. That took some panicked calls to Lenore's mom to get them in safely.

The biggest proof for them, though, was when they solved a school mystery. Mrs. Leary threatened their English class with detention after finding the answers for an upcoming test in one of the classroom's desks.

Cass' heart charged out of her chest even though she was as innocent as a kitten. She looked around the class and saw Mason Danson and Liam Brunaker exchange looks. After class, she followed them around for a few minutes. She heard one of them say he didn't want to get in trouble. She and Lenore confronted him the next day at their lockers.

"Hey, cheaters," Lenore leaned into being the bad cop.

"What are you saying, weirdo?" Liam said.

"Listen, Liam, we're not mad," Cass said, happy to be the good cop. "We just don't want to get detention if you were cheating on Mrs. Leary's test."

"You had detention with Leary last week, who else would have the copy of the teacher's edition, cheater!" Lenore said, trying to intimidate him.

"I don't know! Eddie Ryans was also there. He started detention before me," he let out.

"That's all we needed, thanks Liam!" Cass cheered.

The girls confronted Eddie at the cafeteria during lunch. They set their trays down and sat across from him.

"Hey Eddie, how are you?" Cass smiled.

"Who are you?" he asked.

Lenore banged the table with her fist. "Just admit you cheated on Mrs. Leary's test!" she said, accusingly. "I don't want to be punished because you can't remember the simple plot to *Sleepy Hollow*. If you don't tell her, we will."

English class started that day with Mrs. Leary announcing that the cheater had stepped forward and that she had changed the test questions. Lenore and Cass silently low-fived.

Cass was never more proud of solving that mystery. Life was a little sleepy after that, but her precognition never stopped her from looking out for things.

If only she could share it with her parents.

Chapter Four

Cass' thoughts moved on, and by that Tuesday, she was ready to hang out with Lenore in the trees. The two trudged through the Hurley front door, ready for anything but homework.

"MOOOM, WE'RE HOME," Lenore called from the hallway as she led her friend through the house.

"LIVING ROOM," she heard her mom holler back. "TWINS ARE NAPPING."

Cass and Lenore dropped their backpacks off at the dinner table and went to raid the kitchen pantry for snacks.

"Chips and salsa?" Lenore grabbed a bag.

"Sure," Cass replied as she walked to the fridge, looking for something to drink.

Mrs. Hurley walked in behind them.

"Before you ask, you can go to the woods after you finish homework," she said as if she'd had to say it a hundred times before.

"Like we weren't going to do homework," Lenore chuckled, looking at Cass for help.

"Yeah, Mrs. Hurley, we're responsible and mature," Cass replied as she grabbed chocolate milk out of the fridge.

"Yeah," Lenore said. "Wait, Cass, I think I want to make strawberry milk instead. Do we have the regular stuff?"

Half an hour into doing her math worksheet, Lenore finished and then helped Cass with a few problems. Math came pretty easily to Lenore, which made class boring for her. The teachers were always telling her parents she should test into Algebra class, but then she'd miss her best friend.

Lenore was ecstatic when Cass moved to Moon Town. Most of her elementary school friends had started changing that summer, growing up early and acting like high schoolers with makeup routines and wanting boyfriends. Lenore liked being juvenile and fiercely held on to her childhood innocence. It was a dream come true when Cass had sat next to her in homeroom that first day. She'd never met someone as weird and fun as her.

All her classmates thought it was weird when she'd asked everyone to stop calling her Eleanor and be known as Lenore in fifth grade. While most were spooked out by Edgar Allan Poe, Lenore had known she wanted to change her name when her uncle read "The Raven" to her at a family reunion that year. Her mom rolled her eyes at first, but her Uncle Jack was delighted. The twins might even think Lenore was her actual name.

"Oh! Lenore. Like from 'The Raven'," Cass said when they first exchanged names. "Personally, I like 'The Gold-Bug' best."

Lenore knew they were going to be best friends from then on.

The best part of being friends with Cass was their adventures. They would walk through the woods behind her house and pretend they were on a great adventure. Sometimes it was an easy afternoon of climbing trees, sometimes they maybe counted snakes, other times they pretended they were on a quest to stop the end of the world.

Middle school stunk rotten eggs, but Lenore was glad to have a friend who had her back.

"Okay, so move the X and the number is now…" Lenore started.

"Positive?" Cass asked.

"Yeah," Lenore said.

"Okay, now I subtract this and get three?"

"Yep!"

"Awesome," Cass tucked her homework into her math folder and put it back in her backpack. "Let's go to the woods."

The girls approached Mrs. Hurley, now in the kitchen, thawing meat for dinner.

"All done?" she asked as she chopped vegetables.

"Yes, Mom," Lenore said. "Can we please go outside now?"

"Is your walkie-talkie charged?"

Lenore sighed as she walked over to the charging radios on the kitchen counter and grabbed one.

"Yeah, it's charged. But Mom, when can I get a cell phone?" she whined.

"When you need one. It's not like you can get a signal in the woods, anyways."

"But Cass has a phone!"

"Eleanor Rose, do you want to go outside?"

"Yes, Mom," Lenore gave up. "I'll let you know if anything happens."

"Have fun. I'll reach out to you when it's dinner time."

Cass and Lenore walked out of the house through the living room and slid the back door shut.

"My mom is so annoying," Lenore sighed.

"At least she listens," Cass replied. "My mom only pays attention to Tommy and Lucy. I told her an earthquake destroyed the school on Friday and she went 'That's nice!'"

"Yeah, I can't beat that."

"Want to go climb some trees?"

"Okay."

Chapter Five

The only thing worse than being bored in the woods that day was the rain showers gushing in on Friday, cancelling Cass' cross-country meet. Lenore tried to cheer her up with talks of a sleepover.

"Hey, now you can come to my volleyball game tonight!" Lenore grinned at lunch. "My mom says if I have ten assists I can order a pizza with any toppings I want."

"Why ten assists?"

"Because she keeps going on and on about the importance of teamwork over being the star, or something," Lenore said. "I always contribute, anyways, but I'll definitely do it for my own pizza. Maybe we could split one if you come?"

"Yeah, okay. Let me call my mom after school and see if she'll drop off sleepover stuff."

Lenore held up her bargain with her mom. She had twelve assist sets and scored five points out of the three matches the Aldrin Middle School Moonwalkers won at home. Cass was sad she couldn't race the next day, but was happy to chant *"Pizza! Pizza! Pizza!"* with Lenore on their way home. They enjoyed a half cheese, half pineapple and olive pie as they watched movies in the

Hurley den. The two stayed up late talking until they fell asleep.

***

The next morning, the girls were awoken by Lenore's mom at 10:30. They ate her dad's blueberry pancakes as they started on homework. Cass stared at her Biology assignment, feeling unmotivated until she finally fell into a groove. English vocabulary was next, then History. Then came Math. Cass stared at the first problem for a few minutes, but couldn't make sense of it.

"Hey Lenore, can you help me with this problem?"

"In a few minutes, I'm working on problem ten."

Cass waited in silence for a while as her friend was nose to paper. Her heart started racing, and her stomach hurt.

"Okay, what did you want to show me?" Lenore said, looking up.

"The first problem, but my stomach kind of hurts right now," Cass said. "I feel doom and gloom coming."

"Do you think something's happening out there?" Lenore motioned to the woods outside the sliding glass doors.

"Yeah, maybe."

Lenore bounded to the stairs and shouted up. "Hey Mom, we need to take a break! We're going to go outside!"

"Okay! Grab a radio!" her mom called down.

Cass and Lenore were out the back door a moment later.

"So where is your gut telling you to go?" Lenore asked.

Cass started straight down the trail right in front of them. She led Lenore a hundred feet before turning left and walking a quarter of a mile. Lenore started marking the trees with chalk she'd kept in her pockets so they wouldn't get lost.

After a few more minutes of silence, Lenore finally spoke up.

"Are you feeling any better?"

"No, something bad is going on," Cass said as she grabbed her tingling arm.

"Like maybe some coyote is trying to eat a bunny back here?"

"Maybe?"

"Or vultures fighting over roadkill?"

"Or maybe a serial killer hiding in the woods?"

Lenore laughed. "Cass, there aren't any asylums nearby for looney bins to escape from," Lenore said. "Come on, let's head back. We didn't find anything."

Right then, Cass noticed something blue sticking out of the earth-toned foliage on the forest floor about two hundred feet away. "Hey, what's that?" she asked.

She and Lenore trudged toward the blue bump that grew larger the closer they got. Cass' stomach sank further than she thought possible as she saw something familiar come into focus. Not something—someone. It looked like a pile of clothes. And then they saw a body—a man—covered in freshly fallen leaves. Cass' right arm started shaking as she felt Lenore grab her hand, her own mouth agape. Three bloody wounds stained what they could now see was a navy blue sweater. His shoes were covered in mud, still damp from the night before. His arms were stiff, and his hair was tangled and messy. Cuts on his hands made them look like red gloves. Even without his glasses and blank expression, the girls stared at Edward Benson's corpse for a whole minute as every scenario ran through their heads.

Lenore finally pressed the button on her two-way radio with her free hand.

"Hey, Mom? Are you there? Mom?" Her voice shook.

"Honey, what's wrong? Are you okay?" her mom asked.

"Yeah, we're okay, but we found something."

"What did you find?"

Lenore looked up, meeting Cass' gaze. "I marked our trail on the trees. It might be best for you to see it yourself. Maybe the police too."

Chapter Six

The woods felt somehow more unwelcoming to Cass with police walking around. Crime scene tape was wrapped around trees. CSI was capturing everything that might be used as evidence, and the ambulance and other official vehicles' lights flashed through the trees. Cass felt outside her body there, standing in the leaves next to Lenore and Mrs. Hurley. Her mind wandered as they answered Detective David Gomez's questions. The young Hispanic man stood still in his trench coat and khakis as he wrote in a tiny notebook.

"So, yeah, Cass and I were heading to turn back and we saw a blue lump standing out here, so we approached it," Lenore repeated for what felt like the five hundredth time.

Detective Gomez nodded.

"And then we realized it was Mr. Benson's body, so I grabbed my walkie-talkie—"

"Walkie-talkie?" Gomez asked.

"I make her use a walkie-talkie out here for her safety, detective," Mrs. Hurley answered.

"Not a cell phone?"

Lenore rolled her eyes. "See, mom? This is why I need a

phone! Even the police agree."

"I never said that," Gomez said quickly.

"Lenore, we've talked about this," her mom hissed.

"Please go on, Miss Hurley," Gomez tried to steer the duo back to their conversation.

"Oh, yeah, I grabbed my walkie-talkie and told my mom we'd found something, so she came out here…"

Cass stopped paying attention to the conversation. She started noticing the setting sun, the dark blue fabric of Detective Gomez's tie, the way her toes were starting to tingle with cold, the orange cones outlining where Mr. Benson was found.

"Cass, he was asking you a question." Mrs. Hurley touched her shoulder.

She snapped back to reality. "What was that?"

"What made you aware of the corpse?" Gomez asked.

"Oh, that!" Cass said a little too enthusiastically. *Wait, what if he thinks I did it*, she thought to herself. *That sounded too happy.*

"I just had a feeling that something"—she paused to cut out the word *bad*. Didn't want anyone thinking she was crazy— "something was happening."

Gomez nodded and wrote something down in his notepad. He looked at Mrs. Hurley. "Do you know anyone else in the neighborhood?"

"Us, Mr. Benson, the Starks are further down, as are the Jepsens, but no one seems close enough to where the girls radioed me," she answered. "But the Starks and the Jepsens are pretty old. I don't think they've walked beyond ten feet of their backyards."

The detective wrote some more.

"Is there anything else any of you can tell me?"

"Girls?" Mrs. Hurley prompted.

Cass and Lenore looked down, then around, then at each other.

"He was an old man who liked getting black coffees every Friday at The Roast of Moon Town," Lenore offered.

"We didn't do it, we swear!" Cass pleaded. She was surprised at her own nerves.

"It's okay miss, I don't think there's any evidence to suggest you were here last night when the crime happened," Gomez said. "One more thing." He reached into his trench coat's pocket and pulled out a business card. "Call me if you can remember any more information."

Cass took the card and put it in her pocket with shaking hands. The girls and Mrs. Hurley walked back to the house in silence, the sound of crunched leaves following them. Cass noticed the occasional bird call, wondering if anyone else was trying to take in everything that had happened. Only after getting through the sliding door and into the Hurley abode could the girls feel like breathing again.

"Lenore, Cass, do you want to talk about what happened out there?"

Both girls paused before talking over each other quickly.

"Why was there so much blood?" Cass asked

"Who could carry him out there?" Lenore said.

"Did he meet someone out there?"

"Who would want to kill Mr. Benson?"

"What kind of knife leaves those stabs?"

"What motive is there to kill an old guy?"

"Is his family going to be okay?"

"Does he have a pet who misses him?"

"Okay, okay," Mrs. Hurley put up her hands. "One thing at a time. I'm glad you're both safe, physically. Thank you for reaching out to me to report Mr. Benson. Cass, I'm going to call your parents to let them know what happened. You're more than welcome to stay for dinner. Let us know if you girls need any help emotionally. You saw the dead body of someone you knew. That could be difficult to deal with."

She walked off into another room.

Lenore's dad walked in after putting the twins down for a nap. "Is there anything I can get for you girls? Snacks? Movies? Video games?" he said.

Both girls were quiet. Cass was still trying to stay in the present as she noticed the family pictures on the kitchen walls.

"Hey dad, can we still go out into the woods after this is all done?" Lenore asked. "You know with the police and stuff?"

Her dad hesitated. "I don't know, honey. We want you to be safe, but for now let's say no more adventures until the police conclude their investigation," he said.

The girls were silent.

"Do you want to talk to a counselor?"

Both were still silent.

"Can we watch a movie that doesn't involve someone dying?" Cass asked.

"Uh," Lenore's dad said.

"Yeah no murder mysteries, maybe something light like *The Hobbit*. Can you make us popcorn, Dad?" Lenore asked.

"Sure."

Chapter Seven

Cass was still exhausted that Monday from everything that happened over the weekend. She was looking forward to seeing Lenore again to break the tension in her head, but when she got to the locker room that morning, her friend was nowhere in sight. Her classmates all waved, unaware of the murder in the woods. Cass still waited for Lenore as more and more girls filtered in, but she never showed.

As the class bell rang, Cass walked into the gym hoping Lenore would still make it to school. She did not.

Cass went about her day hoping to see Lenore, but gave up that hope by lunch. As she wandered around the cafeteria, she found a seat by Jada Lewis and some of her other cross-country teammates.

"Hey, Cass, how was your weekend?" Jada asked.

"It was something. I wish our meet hadn't been cancelled," she sighed. "I was ready to make up for last weekend."

"Don't worry about it!" Emma Stanwell, another teammate, patted her on the back.

"Hey, did you hear about the murder that happened this

weekend?" Jada interrupted. "My family saw it in the news!"

Jada looked around for lunch monitors, then pulled out her phone from her jacket when it seemed the coast was clear. She typed some things in, then a local news website story appeared on the screen. She handed it to Cass. She stared at it while holding her half-bitten apple. It was a short story.

First murder in Moon Town occurs Saturday

"An elderly man's body was found stabbed three times in the woods near the 4500 block of Hayes Road on Saturday morning. According to police, two minors were walking in the woods when they discovered the body, identified as Edward Benson, 82.

'We've identified the stab wounds from a kitchen knife and believe the victim's body was dragged out to the woods Friday night,' Moon Town Police Detective David Gomez said. 'It was good luck that we found the body sooner rather than later, which will help us figure out what happened. We could use all the information anyone has.'

Anyone with information is encouraged to contact the police at (412) 555-9089 or at tips@policeemail.com."

"Wow," Cass did a double take.

"That's not all. The local news stations all did stories on it, and I think I saw Lenore's parents being interviewed on one of them," Jada said. "Isn't that where Lenore lives?"

"Yeah she's neighbors with Mr. Benson," Cass said.

"So was it you two who found the body?" Her jaw dropped.

"Yeah."

"Whoa! What happened?" Emma asked.

"We were just walking in the woods, and when we were turning back to Lenore's house we noticed a figure in the trees that wasn't moving."

"What did it look like," Emma whispered. "The corpse, I mean."

"Um, it was kind of pale and there were blood stains, but it mostly looked like he was sleeping," Cass said.

The rest of the girls at the table stared at her. Half of them looked sick, the other half looked like they wanted more information. Katie Krombie, green in the face again, got up from the table and left.

"What?" Cass asked as she looked around at the remaining girls.

"Who do you think did it?" Jada asked. "Is there anyone out there? If it's not been solved yet, I think it's a cold case."

"I don't know," Cass said, feeling overwhelmed. She hadn't slept well the last two nights due to the image of the dead body haunting her dreams in addition to her usual insomnia. "Guys, can we switch topics?"

"Oh, okay," Emma said. "So did you watch the new episode of *Greendale*? I can't believe they just tease Jeff and Annie so much."

"*Greendale*?" Katie asked as she sat back down at the table. Everyone started talking about who they shipped on the show, and Cass was happy for the distraction as she poked at the rest of her lunch.

Chapter Eight

Cass ran from all her feelings that afternoon at cross-country practice. She put so much focus into her running she outpaced half the boys on the team.

"Fairchild!" Coach Webber called as Cass finished another lap around the track. "You're going too fast. Stop overdoing it."

"But I just have so much energy to get out, Coach," she pleaded. "The end of the season is coming up, anyway."

"And we don't need someone who overdid themselves in practice to get injured on race day. Go do some jumping jacks while we wait for the rest of the team to finish," Coach Webber said.

Cass didn't let it bother her as she started on her jumping jacks for the rest of practice.

The physical exertion lulled Cass into feeling calm after that. But it all left her body when she saw Lenore the next morning in the locker room.

"Lenore!" she squealed as she hugged her friend. "I missed you!"

"I missed you too," Lenore said as she returned the hug. "My parents made me go to counseling yesterday, and then made me stay home because the media circus is going nuts near the crime scene. They figured our classmates would have heard about it from their parents too, and everyone would be bothering me at school."

"Okay, but I had to answer everyone's questions at lunch without you," Cass sighed.

"That's rough, buddy."

"Tell me about it. I don't want to get asked to describe what a dead body looks like anymore."

The girls walked into the gym, ready for class to start. After the Pledge of Allegiance, however, both girls were pulled to the front office. They both sat confused in guidance counselor Jen Barber's office.

Cass looked around. There was one aqua-colored accent wall behind Miss Barber's desk. The school guidance counselor had a mug with smiley faces filled to the brim with pens and little trinkets on her desk. The large tissue box was covered in yarn, as if she liked to decorate to invite kids to cry. Lenore was trying not to smirk at the inspirational posters with whales and bald eagles on them. Cass felt weird sitting in a half round aqua-colored chair instead of the usual plastic school seat. The purple orchid in the window and small, planted money tree in the office corner did nothing for them.

"So, you're both not in trouble," Miss Barber started as she sat down in her correct posture chair. She was a woman in her late twenties with green eyes and auburn hair pulled into a stylish messy bun. Her deep pink lipstick was applied a little too wide as she smiled like she had everything under control.

"But we heard about what happened to you this weekend and wanted you to talk to us about it."

Lenore did her best not to roll her eyes.

"I just went to counseling yesterday," she complained. "It was very weird, a little frightening, and it was awkward dealing with the police. Yes, I'm a little worried since I found a neighbor I barely talked to dead. But I also know he was old and lonely, anyway, and all he seemed to want was one black coffee every Friday. Can I please go?"

"Lenore, please use your manners when you speak to adults," Miss Barber said. "You both went through something that children should never experience. We don't want the unfortunate experience to carry into your classroom performances. Cass, how are you doing?"

The room was feeling a little warm for Cass. She didn't want Miss Barber worrying over her and poking into her life. What if she discovered Cass' psychic powers? On the other hand, she *was* really stressed from all of this. Maybe talking to someone would help.

"Well, I keep seeing his body on the ground when I close my eyes," Cass murmured. "And I just can't stop thinking about him. Lenore and I used to trick-or-treat at his house. He would give us butterscotch candy that always tasted stale. And the only other time we saw him was whenever we went to the coffee shop. He glared at everyone and always ordered the same small plain coffee. I just feel so sad, but I didn't know him at the same time. We never knew his family, or saw them. Was he lonely? Did he die alone? Why would someone stab him…"

Cass began crying, and her words became harder to understand. Barber handed her the decorated tissue box and let her wail it out. Lenore rubbed her hand against Cass' back. After five minutes of ugly crying, Miss Barber spoke up.

"Cass, it seems you may have made an attachment to Edward Benson. While there's not a lot you can do to get to know him now, have you considered going to his funeral?"

"What?" Cass sniffled as she looked up at the adult.

Miss Barber turned to her computer and typed for thirty seconds as the two girls exchanged glances.

"Here, let's find his obituary and see when and where the funeral is. You can meet his family and friends who attend and learn more about him. If it's before Saturday, I'll write you both excused absences."

Chapter Nine

Incense filled the air at St. Mark's Episcopal Church. The stained glass windows shone the autumn light through the gray stone. The wooden pews and matching stone flooring added to the uneasy feel of the church. The giant organ in the choir loft was the bow on the present of it all for Cass, although there was a person in black playing the piano by the altar.

As Cass, Lenore, and Miss Barber took their seats in a middle pew, the girls started watching and taking in everyone else in attendance. The pianist by the altar was in his sixties, and completely bald as he bent forward playing "Amazing Grace" on repeat. Most people were funeral-ready, dressed in black and dark blue. Cass felt self-conscious wearing a dark gray cotton skirt, black blouse, and heather gray cardigan she'd borrowed from her mom. She looked at Lenore in her all-black skirt and blouse combo. It came with the territory of changing your name to something macabre.

Cass looked around at the twenty people in attendance. Most of them were older, like Mr. Benson. Lenore nudged Cass and pointed out her neighbors, the Starks and the Jepsens, near the front. The foursome sitting together looked stern as they stared straight forward. A few people Cass didn't know sat near them. They looked a little sad.

Cass caught Miss Barber looking at someone catty-corner from their pew. Her gaze lasted a little too long. It was none other than Detective Gomez, in a black tie and dark pants. He turned around after a few seconds, spotted the girls, and waved at them as he caught their glances.

Cass was flooded with relief once the funeral began; she stared at the program, which had been handed to her earlier. Mr. Benson apparently had two children—both married—and had four grandchildren.

She felt herself rocking a bit during the readings about death until she felt Miss Barber firmly place her hand on her shoulder to stop her. It felt so weird to hear someone call death "a way home." Cass' family was Catholic, and while they attended Mass every Sunday, the thought of dying still terrified her. She liked the image of Heaven as a place up in the sky where you see your family and friends after you all die, but she was not ready to go, or for anyone she knew to go yet.

Cass was reassured that the funeral was closed-casket—she didn't want to see Mr. Benson's face again. She imagined others there would have also felt a little sick seeing all the stab wounds. Would a mortician have cleaned it all up? Would his family have paid for that?

It was so foreign going from seeing the same old man every so often at a coffee shop, alive and well, to then seeing his corpse covered in fallen leaves from the night before.

Cass looked at Lenore, who was staring at her nails as the priest talked and talked. Her best friend was a tough nut when it came to the macabre and grotesque, but she wondered if Lenore was actually fine, or possibly faking it so she could move on quicker.

The Mass went on quickly, and the girls were wondering what was left when the priest said Mr. Benson's son Ted would give a quick eulogy since the family had passed on a wake.

A thin middle-aged man in a charcoal sportcoat and onyx tie slowly walked up to the lectern. He sighed before starting.

"Hello, everyone, I am Ted, Edward's son. Let's get this over with," he sighed again. "Edward Matthew Benson was born on June 4, 1943 in Danville, Kentucky. He grew up with two older brothers and three younger sisters, all of whom couldn't make it today. He was active in the sports scene and played quarterback for the Danville High School football team. He also played basketball and baseball for the school, and took them to two state championships for baseball.

He later went on to play football for Louisville and stayed there to work in construction. While he was there, he fell in love with our mom Margie, and the two got married in 1965.

As they moved back to Danville, dearest Dad started a construction company to build houses for those without the means to buy a home. If you came to him and couldn't pay for construction upfront, he would try to meet you halfway. His initiative drew in so many people, you could say he built half the houses in that city. And while he was building those houses, he was ignoring the time he could've spent with his kids by either being out at the bar with friends or the lake fishing alone.

"He finally retired in 2000, and with all that extra time he could have spent with us or his wife of thirty-five years, he still decided to spend it all at the lake fishing. And then when his beloved wife died of cancer in 2008, you know how he helped support the family? By moving all the way out to Moon Town and ignoring us, refusing to come home for the holidays or inviting us out here. What a great father he was." Ted rolled his eyes as some people gasped.

"Well, Dad, now you're dead, and you have to see us. Is that too much for you? Good riddance."

Ted Jr. traipsed off the podium and—to everyone's shock—stormed straight out of the church. Cass and Lenore stared at Miss Barber, whose mouth was agape. The pallbearers picked up the casket and walked out of the church as the pianist awkwardly rushed to play an old Christian tune.

"So, should we go to the reception?" Miss Barber asked the girls.

Cass tugged at her mom's cardigan, and Lenore awkwardly fidgeted with her friendship bracelet as they waited for Mr. Benson's family to arrive at the reception hall. His grave was only a few miles from the church. Both were avoiding people when Detective Gomez approached their group.

"Hello, ladies, how are you?" he asked cooly.

"Hi, sir," Cass said quickly, straightening up.

"Good," Lenore said. "Why are you here? Searching for the murderer at the funeral? Do police have no decency these days?"

Gomez cracked a smile.

"I hope I have plenty of decency, Miss Hurley," he said. "I personally attend the victim's funerals when I can, offer the family support, and let them know the force is here for them. What are you two doing here?"

"I brought them so they can experience some closure," Miss Barber said as she excitedly extended her hand. "Hi, I'm Jennifer Barber, Moon Town Middle School guidance counselor. But you can call me Jen. And your name, sir?"

"Detective David Gomez," he introduced himself as he felt her enthusiastic handshake.

He casually chatted with Miss Barber. She talked a little too excitedly for someone who was at a funeral. Cass and Lenore snickered for a while as family members began trickling into the hall.

When people finally started sitting, Lenore and Cass tried seating themselves with her neighbors, but Miss Barber kept pushing them to meet Mr. Benson's family. They found themselves confused, standing in front of Mr. Benson's daughter Allison, and her husband Ken.

"We're so sorry about that eulogy. My brother is just kind of sore about everything," Allison started as she picked at her table salad. "So how did you know my father?"

"I was sort of neighbors with him," Lenore said into her cup of lemonade.

"And I'm the best friend," Cass mumbled. "Lenore's, not your dad's," she then blurted out.

Everyone at the table smiled a little.

"Girls, speak up for yourselves," Miss Barber said. "These two were the ones who reported his body in the woods. They were out for a walk when they found him."

"Really?" Allison's eyes got bigger. "Thank you so much. It's horrible what happened to Dad, but we're glad someone found him sooner than later. Did you know him well?"

"Not really," Lenore said. "We only saw him at our favorite coffee shop."

Cass shook her head. "No."

"Hey girls, why don't you tell them a nice memory you have with Mr. Benson?" Miss Barber encouraged them.

Both girls stood silent for a minute trying to think of any time they spent with him.

"One Halloween he gave me two butterscotch candies because he liked my Supreme Court Justice costume, even if he did call me a church choir member," Lenore said. "I guess I impressed him, so that was cool."

"One time at The Roast of Moon Town he saw me grab a unicorn frappe and said it was very colorful," Cass offered. "He also said it matched me, which was true because I was wearing a blue and pink shirt that day."

The adults stared at the girls for a few seconds. Allison eventually broke a small smile.

"Well, thank you for those stories," Allison said. "Dad was nothing if not a little aloof. Not that there's anything wrong with it!"

Allison and others started talking amongst themselves as Miss Barber got up from the table for more lemonade. The girls breathed a sigh of relief at getting a break from Miss Barber closely watching them, as she was now chatting up the detective again.

"Something doesn't feel right," Lenore whispered to Cass.

"I know what you mean. I don't think the detective is being totally honest with us," Cass whispered back. "Also, why was Mr. Benson's son so…" she couldn't think of another word.

"Rude? Abrupt? Cranky? All three?" Lenore offered. "Could his son have been out here the night of the murder?" Lenore said.

"Could any of the people in this room have been?"

"Want to investigate a little?"

The girls walked up to the table with Lenore's neighbors, the Starks and Jepsens, who were chatting away. Both sets of her older neighbors were quietly nodding at each other and making small talk when Mrs. Sherri Jepsen saw the girls and turned.

"Lenore, it's so good to see you," Mrs. Jepsen smiled. "I'm surprised you made it."

"Well, when you find what we did in the woods, it's kind of necessary to go to these things. At least, according to our counselor."

"We're happy to be here," Cass spoke up. "We didn't really know Mr. Benson well. Did you guys know him?"

Mrs. Jepsen's lip turned up slightly before her husband interrupted her.

"We knew him a little," John Jepsen said. "Every few months he'd come over and tell us fishing tales over a trout dinner. His son isn't wrong about his love of fishing, apparently."

"We also went to church with him. Saw him here every Sunday. He rarely stuck around for the Sunday social afterwards, though," Mrs. Alexandra Stark said.

"We don't mean to hurt anyone's feelings, but was Mr. Benson rich or something? Why would anyone want to kill him?" Lenore asked.

"He had little money, dear," Mrs. Stark said. "We're just as confused as you are as to why someone would kill him."

"But do you think there's something suspicious going on right here and now? Like could the killer be here?" Lenore asked.

Her neighbors loudly laughed at her suggestion.

"Honey, why would a murderer go to their victim's funeral?" Mrs. Jepsen asked. "Isn't that a little too on the nose?"

"Because they're covering their tracks by pretending they cared for him," Lenore offered.

"Right, right, but there's also a policeman here. Wouldn't that make them nervous?" Mr. Jepsen asked.

"Not if they're a good liar," Lenore said.

"They could also be showboating to the police that they did it, but there's no evidence to turn them in," Cass said.

"You two have been reading too many books," Mr. Jepsen said with a smile.

"I think it's noble that you're trying to help," Mrs. Jepsen said. "Mr. Benson was a small but special part of the community."

Before the girls could respond, Mr. Benson's family members began arguing loudly. Every head turned to them.

"I'M NOT TAKING THEM! I DON'T WANT ANYTHING FROM HIM!" Ted Jr. yelled. "He never gave me *anything* else after I grew up! Why would I take anything now?"

"Ted, we've talked about this. Emma is allergic to cat dander!" Allison hurled back.

"SEND THEM TO THE SHELTER FOR ALL I CARE!"

"They'll get put down! I don't want them to be like Dad!"

Cass and Lenore gasped at the argument, and looked at each other for a moment. They knew what to do. They slowly approached Miss Barber, who was still next to Detective Gomez.

"Miss Barber, I think we can help them," Cass addressed her with big eyes.

✳✳✳

Later that day, Lenore burst into her house holding the fluffiest white Ragdoll in her arms like a baby. Cass followed behind her holding a gray Maine Coon like a football. They walked into the front room to find Lenore's mom working at the computer. She stopped typing almost immediately, eyes wide as she tried to take in what she was seeing.

"Hey, Mom, this is Murphy, one of Mr. Benson's cats," Lenore began. "His children didn't want his cats and kept arguing about it at the funeral reception, so we stepped in to save them from the local kill shelter. The family agreed to give us all the pet supplies in the house, so we already have food bowls, litter boxes, and toys. They're in Miss Barber's car. Murphy loves ear scratches and being called a baby. Also, Miss Barber said we should keep them as a way to connect with our trauma, and that cats help with mental health. Therefore, we have to keep him."

Mrs. Hurley sighed as she face-palmed.

Chapter Ten

"Whatcha got there?" Cass' mom asked as Cass walked in that afternoon with her new cat.

"Mom, this is Elroy," Cass passed the cat to her mom. "Elroy, this is Mom! Mr. Benson apparently had two cats when he died, and his kids didn't want to take them. So, Lenore and I volunteered to save them from a kill shelter. I have his cat box and bowls and stuff in Miss Barber's car, if you want to help bring them in. And before you say no, cats are very good for mental health and closure and stuff."

"Okay," her mom agreed, handing Elroy back to Cass and walking out to the car to get the supplies. Right then, Tommy ran up to the new cat and got in its face. Elroy squirmed in fear.

"Who's the cat?" he asked.

"Tommy, this is Elroy," Cass said, introducing them

"Yay! We have a pet," he cheered.

"No, *I* have a pet," Cass corrected.

"NO! I want him too!"

Elroy started squiggling in Cass' arms. He wanted out.

"You wouldn't take care of him!"

"Stop arguing," their mom intervened as she carried in cat

box supplies. "Now go grab the rest of his supplies from the van, kids."

Cass gently put Elroy on the ground. He froze in fear of his new surroundings. The siblings continued arguing under their breath for the next few minutes. Once everything was in the house, Miss Barber drove away, and Cass got back to holding her new fluffy cat, who was still afraid on the staircase.

Her dad pulled up after his day at work right then.

"Hey, kids," he said as he entered the hall.

"Dad!" Tommy yelled, running up to hug him.

"Hey, Dad," Cass said, still holding her companion.

"What's this?" her dad said as he scratched Elroy behind the ears.

"Cass got a cat from Mr. Benson, apparently," Mrs. Fairchild said.

"And don't worry, he's *my* responsibility," Cass emphasized as she stared at her brother.

"That's not fair!"

"Nor was Mr. Benson getting a knife to the chest three times," Cass said, glaring at her brother. "But here we are."

Tommy started crying, and her parents made Cass apologize.

Later at dinner, Mr. Fairchild agreed she could keep Elroy if she cleaned his box, cut his nails, and fed him. They shook hands in agreement.

"But how do you really feel about the name Elroy?" her father asked.

"That's what he responds to," Cass shrugged.

"Well, he was owned by an old man."

"Be glad I let Lenore take the white Ragdoll he named Murphy."

Mr. Fairchild gawked at the thought of white cat hair all over the house. "Thank you for dodging that bullet!" he laughed.

"So, how was the funeral?" her mom asked.

"It was fine," Cass said. She realized she was still wearing her mom's clothes, and put the cardigan on the back of her chair.

"There weren't a lot of people."

"You and Lenore always said he seemed lonely."

"Yeah, but then his son gave, like, the worst eulogy ever. He named every one of his dad's accomplishments, but then also basically said he sucked."

"Language, Cassandra Felicity," Mrs. Fairchild said as she turned to Tommy, making a face so he wouldn't copy her. Cass rolled her eyes.

"Sorry, but the point is, it seems like his kids didn't like him, even though he was murdered."

"Sometimes families can be complicated," her dad said. "We see this all the time at the hospital. Adult children get mad at their parents for having procedures without telling them or disagreeing with their decisions. There was probably way more going on behind the scenes than what they were letting on at the funeral."

"Yeah, but it's all just been so weird," Cass started. "I mean, Tommy is annoying, but if he died, I'd be sad."

"Thank you, Cass!" Tommy interrupted. "If you died, I would cry a little, too, then probably turn your room into my game room."

Cass made a face. Before she could respond, her mom changed the subject.

"So, what do you kids want to do for Halloween? I assume we're taking Lenore around the block since her neighborhood has all this ongoing drama."

Cass excused herself from the dinner table and went to her room. She sat on the floor with her back against her bed and took a few breaths. She wasn't quite ready to do any homework, or anything for that matter. She was absolutely stuck. After zoning out for five minutes, something fuzzy rubbed its head against her right elbow.

Elroy was rubbing his head on her, and she opened her hand and started petting him. He must have run up to her room to hide after meeting Dad. He started purring and walking around her room, rubbing himself against her bed stand and desk. He got under her desk and laid on his side, paws close to his body with his stomach out to her.

"Hey, Elroy," she said softly. She reached her hand out to pet his belly, but stopped. What if he attacked her? *Eh, the risk is worth the reward.* She petted his belly, and he started meowing loudly.

"What a good boy!" she smiled.

Tommy poked his head through the door.

"Good boy? I want to pet him!" He hurried to the cat who then dove under Cass' bed.

"Get out of my room!" Cass yelled.

Cass went to bed with mixed thoughts of the day. She was glad to have missed class, but what if she fell behind? Also, while she understood being annoyed at her father from time to time, why was Mr. Benson's son so rude when he was talking about him?

Cass' dad worked odd and long hours at the hospital, but she didn't resent him for missing her class programs or anything. He tried his best to make it to her meets. If he was murdered, her eulogy for him would be talking about what a fun and supportive dad he was.

Seeing Detective Gomez there also felt wrong. Maybe he was trying to solve the case there… Also, Miss Barber was clearly into him. Did detectives know when people were hitting on them?

Also, what was with Lenore's neighbors acting like they were children, and like there wasn't anything suspicious going on? Their neighbor was basically found in their collective backyard with blood staining his sweater. It was creepy.

And then, what about the cats?

Cass started to worry she couldn't take care of Elroy. She was twelve. She had never taken care of a pet before! On the way to Mr. Benson's house, Miss Barber told them cat care was really basic. What if Elroy got mad at her one day and peed on her shoes, or chewed up her ribbon bookmarks?

As she finally started to drift off, Cass startled when something jumped on the bed. She almost screamed until Elroy settled himself next to her legs, curled into a ball, and went to sleep.

Cass was jealous he could fall asleep so suddenly while her mind kept wandering. Her brain jumped tracks, back to thinking about school. What if she had another math pop quiz on Thursday? And she failed because she missed what the class learned today?

Then she'd have to repeat seventh grade all over again. Suddenly Cass' right arm started tingling.

What now? She thought as she made up possible reasons for the pain. Maybe something happened at school?

She couldn't control that. She'd double down her studying efforts tomorrow. Cass began praying for the pain in her arm to go away as she drifted off to sleep.

Chapter Eleven

"So, do you think you'll keep Elroy's name?" Lenore asked Cass as they waited for their smoothie that Friday at The Roast of Moon Town.

"Yeah, probably since he knows it," Cass replied. "You're not thinking of renaming Murphy are you?"

"But how cute would it be to have a cat named Merlin?" Lenore asked. "Or Sherlock? Or Edgar? Or Allan? Or Poe?"

"Don't name your cat Edgar Allan Poe, Lenore, that's too on the nose," Cass laughed.

They finally got their smoothies and were walking to Mrs. Hurley when they stopped at the sight of Ted Benson, Jr. walking in and ordering at the counter. The two were staring a little too hard from the old couch when he caught their stares, and walked up to them.

"Hey there," he said, casually. "So, you were the people who found my father's body in the woods?"

"Um," Cass said, still trying to process what was happening.

"Yes," Lenore asserted. "And you gave a harsh eulogy at the end of his funeral."

He stared at them.

"So, what are your names?" He held out his hand to shake theirs.

Mrs. Hurley coughed as she approached the man.

"Marie Hurley," she said. "Why are you speaking to my daughter and her best friend?"

"I'm sorry. I'm Ted Benson, and I believe these girls found my father—"

He was cut off by the barista.

"One black coffee for Ted!" He turned around and got his coffee.

"That's funny, your dad always ordered the same drink here," Lenore perked up.

"Pardon?" He turned around.

"Your dad was usually here every Friday afternoon, and he always ordered a small black coffee, just like you"

"Very observant."

"Well, this is our favorite place," she said as she casually gestured to Cass.

"Yeah, but he usually kept to himself and stared out the window the whole time," Cass added.

"I'm so sorry, they just really like people watching and 'having adventures,'" Mrs. Hurley added with air quotes. "They've read so many novels, they think life is a book itself. If you're not waiting for someone here, do you want to join us?"

"I'm waiting for my sister to text me when she's ready to go to my dad's house and go through his stuff," Ted said as he reached for his cell phone. "His will was very scant. We both get the house and what's left of his bank account, but there's nothing to his personal possessions. I have a feeling I won't like his stuff."

Cass and Lenore exchanged looks, but weren't sure what to say.

"I'm sorry about your loss, Ted," Mrs. Hurley said. "If you're here for a while, let us know what we can do to help."

"Actually, would you want to go through his stuff with us? Since the girls took his cats yesterday, there might be some more things that interest them," he asked.

Mrs. Hurley looked at them.

"Well, girls?"

Chapter Twelve

Mr. Benson's house could be full of clues, and for that, Cass and Lenore were excited. That also meant they could be visiting the scene of a murder, and neither were sure how to prepare. Cass pictured old paintings hanging off Mr. Benson's walls, blood stains marking a trail his body made to his deathly exit, and knives all over the counter. Her heart raced as they were about to enter the old brick laid two-story house. She and Lenore hadn't even entered the porch when Ted Jr. and Allison got the cats and their supplies. Was it too gruesome for them to visit the first time?

Cass and Lenore were quick to get out of the Hurley minivan and into the house as soon as they saw Ted unlock the front door.

"Just let us know what you want," he said as they walked into the living room.

Cass made a beeline to the kitchen, and Lenore took her time walking around.

Cass did a double take at how normal the place looked. The walls were clean, the kitchen was spotless aside from some spilled coffee grounds, and all knives were in their knife block.

She opened a cabinet that revealed six different french presses. She didn't know he liked coffee that much! What else did she not know about him?

Cass started going through utensil drawers when she heard Lenore scream.

"Oh my gosh, Cass! Get in here!"

Cass ran to the living room, confused why her friend was grinning until she handed her framed professional photos of Mr. Benson with his cats. He was sitting in a recliner with Murphy seated on the headrest behind him and Elroy on his lap. Even the cats seemed to be looking at the camera. Cass laughed.

"We need to keep these."

"Yeah," Cass agreed. "I searched the kitchen again and couldn't find anything. It's absolutely spotless."

"That's lame."

"Yeah, hopefully we get something more than cat photos soon."

"There could have been more murder weapons, like in *Clue*. Like a wrench or candle stick or something."

"Lenore, remember he was stabbed. Those wouldn't leave the same injuries."

"Yeah, true," Lenore put the photos under her arm. "Where else should we search?"

"Your mom is still in the library looking at some books, maybe check the bedrooms with Ted and Allison?"

Cass and Lenore walked upstairs and ducked into a guest bedroom after hearing Ted and Allison arguing. The guest bedroom was plain with blue paint, a matching bed set of old blue flowers with a brown headrest, and an empty closet.

"All this points to is that he was an old man who was kind of boring," Lenore complained. "I'm going to check his library with mom and see if he had any good or hollowed-out books."

"I'll catch up to you, I have to go to the bathroom," Cass said as she headed down the hall.

As Cass washed her hands, she looked for a hand towel to dry them on, but the hanger was empty. She sighed as she flicked her hands in the sink and tried to see if the sink's drawers had any towels. The top one had plenty of mini toothpaste bottles, floss, and brushes. Cass went for the second drawer and found a few cotton swabs. At this point, finding a hand towel seemed like less of a possibility, but she pulled the third drawer open, anyways. She gasped a little when she pulled out a long gold necklace with rubies, a single ruby earring, and a gold bracelet.

Curiosity led her to opening the mirror cabinet, eyeing the dark red lipstick tube next to what looked like a case of well-worn blush.

Did Mr. Benson have a lady caller, or did he like dressing up like a woman?

Cass left the bathroom and heard Ted and Allison continuing their argument in the kitchen. She went into Mr. Benson's bedroom and searched the closet. No dresses. She saw some long silver hairs on his dark sports coat that were too long to be Murphy or Elroy's. The bedroom was a boring cream color with sage green sheets and a light wooden headboard. There were, curiously enough, two nightstands—one on each side of the bed. She found the matching earring in the nightstand closer to the window. Cass went through it, upset she didn't find a diary or something else that could easily explain everything that happened to Mr. Benson leading up to his murder. But she was surprised to find a Bible in a drawer. Separate tabs marked different places in the book.

Mr. Benson also kept his heartburn medication on a second bedside table with his alarm clock. Dust was collecting on a half-sipped glass of water. So, this was what the mysterious Edward Benson was all about. Drank water at night, read a Bible, and probably had a girlfriend his kids didn't know about until now—if they were paying attention to the objects in his house.

"Cass! We're going soon," Mrs. Hurley called from downstairs.

Without thinking, Cass grabbed the Bible and shoved the jewelry in her purse, then trotted down the stairs. Lenore could be heard going back and forth with her mom.

"We're not taking that photo," Mrs. Hurley said.

"But, Mom! It's his cats! We can scrapbook it!"

"Eleanor Rose Hurley, that was a man's private possession, and you're not going to flaunt it around school like it's a joke!"

"Scrapbooking isn't a joke, and also, I would do a page for just Merlin! He's so cute! He's family now."

"Merlin?"

"I was thinking of renaming him."

"Honestly, anything you can get off our hands would be great," Ted butted in.

As he started thanking Mrs. Hurley for coming over, Lenore slipped the photo into Cass' tote bag. The two nodded in secret agreement. Cass may need to hold onto the cat pics for a few weeks before they could make their way to the Hurley home.

Mrs. Hurley turned to the girls. "Did you find anything, Cass?"

"Um, I found this Bible," Cass began. "It looks like it was well-read and loved."

"That's nice," Mrs. Hurley said. "Lenore, did you take back that awful photo of yours?"

"Yes, ma'am!" Lenore lied. "But I'm taking his classic editions of *Wuthering Heights* and *Frankenstein*."

"Those you can part with."

The girls' eyes met, as they hoped Mrs. Hurley wouldn't notice.

CHAPTER THIRTEEN

Cass and Lenore passed notes in elvish on their way home, using their shared composition notebook. One would furiously scribble, then low-handedly pass the notebook as Mrs. Hurley kept driving.

"Girls. I know you're talking about what you saw," Mrs. Hurley announced a few miles into the drive home. "If it's really important, please just speak up."
Both stayed silent the rest of the way, and Cass put the notebook in her tote bag. As soon as they opened the door to Lenore's house, they ran upstairs to her room and locked the door.

"So you really found jewelry in his bathroom?" Lenore asked.

"Yeah, it was weird how he just had that one set and then some makeup," Cass said, pulling them out of her tote. "I searched his closets and couldn't find any feminine clothing, so I don't think he was dressing up. He also had two night stands, which was weird. The second earring was in one of them. But my heart was racing before we went into the house, and then again trying to get into his bedroom after his kids left. So, I think it's a good sign we found these."

"Good job!" Lenore cheered. "So, he was a player?"

"I guess," Cass said. "But one set of makeup might mean it was one woman."

"Look at Mr. Benson go, even in his eighties," Lenore said. She walked over to her friend's purse and grabbed the photo of Mr. Benson with his cats out, then opened the back of the picture frame. All that was written on the back was "me and the boys."

"Weird," Lenore said, sliding the photo under her bed. She hid the frame in her closet.

"So weird," Cass said.

"So, did he mark anything in his Bible?"

"I mean, the bookmarks go to Genesis, Leviticus, John, and Acts. I don't really see a pattern here. I think he just liked reading the Bible. Any meaning in your books?"

"No, I just liked the look of these two," Lenore sighed. She put the new copies on her bookshelf. "The library was dusty, but there weren't any obvious clues there like old letters, a writing station, or a fireplace. It was just books, an old leather chair, a lamp, and a lot of cat hair."

"Maybe Mr. Benson was really just a boring, normal guy with a girlfriend."

"Why would a boring, normal guy get murdered in the woods?"

"I don't know."

"Let's try investigating with the jewelry lead."

"Was it just me or are his children kinda weird?" Cass changed the subject.

"Yeah it feels like they really didn't like him, even before he died."

"I wonder when Ted got into town," Cass said.

"Are you calling him a suspect?"

"Wouldn't you?"

Lenore got up from her desk chair and left the room, then came back a minute later with a clean composition notebook. She grabbed a black ink pen from her desk.

"So, this case is unlike anything we've ever solved. It

deserves its own notebook."

"Alright!" Cass cheered. "Where do we start?"

"Let's write what we know: According to the police report, Mr. Benson was killed Friday night, but his body was discovered Saturday morning. Three stab markings from a knife... His knives were all there, in his own kitchen, so it had to be the murderer's. Also, no blood stains in the house. As far as suspects go, his son has a lot of anger toward him. But we also don't know when he showed up in town. My neighbors could be suspects."

"And as far as clues," Cass joined in, "we know he may have a girlfriend, but we didn't see any woman speak up at his funeral. Maybe she was a secret girlfriend, or just a love affair… So, what now?"

"We keep investigating."

Chapter Fourteen

Lenore usually liked attention, but mostly when it came to her grades and athletic abilities. She did not like the attention that came with sitting in offices and talking to adults. Growing up and talking about responsibility and feelings were boring. She'd rather be investigating. Sadly for her, she was facing the second kind of attention with Cass as they sat at Miss Barber's office again that Monday morning.

Miss Barber gave her a calm smile that made her want to roll her eyes. She could tell the counselor wanted something.

"So, girls, how are we feeling today? How are your cats doing?"

"Good," Lenore spoke up first. "Dupin—I renamed him—loves bothering my mom when she's typing, and the twins like chasing him around. He'll sit next to me on the couch even though he's not recognizing his new name."

"Elroy is good," Cass said. "He won't come out from under the bed until night time when he decides to sit on my legs."

"I know the funeral was a lot to take in with that son's, um, creative eulogy and the police being there, but are you worried about anything else?" Miss Barber continued.

She was searching for eye contact. Lenore decided to play along.

"No, and in fact, he actually invited us to see Mr. Benson's house on Saturday," Lenore said.

"He did?"

"Yeah, and he let us take whatever we wanted from it."

Miss Barber stared at them for a few seconds. Lenore was happy to see Miss Barber thrown off her rote of prying questions.

"And how'd that go?"

"Well, we found a lady's jewelry in the bathroom, so we think he had a girlfriend," Cass said. "But we're becoming more convinced that Mr. Benson had an affair, and maybe his son wasn't happy about it. We jotted both things down into our mystery notebook."

"A mystery notebook?"

"Yeah, when we investigate stuff, we write our observations in a notebook until we solve the crime, basically," Lenore said.

Miss Barber took a deep breath. *Did they say something wrong?* Cass worried.

"Girls," she began. "I understand, being so close to this crime, you might feel like you have a duty to solve it, but under no circumstance should you investigate this. Leave this work to the police."

"Why? They haven't gotten any closer to solving it for all we know," Lenore said.

"Yeah, we're fine mental health-wise now," Cass lied. She reached for her right arm and started massaging it. Cass straightened up in her chair, and Lenore followed her.

"Girls, for all we know a serial killer is on the loose," Miss Barber said. "You need to look at this from an adult's perspective—a man was killed in the woods. If someone else suspected you were digging into this, you would be put in harm's way. What would your parents do if you were murdered?"

"Save my clothes as hand-me-downs for my twin sisters," Lenore sarcastically remarked. "But really, Miss Barber, to be a serial killer you have to kill three people within a month, and there's been no murders in Alleghany County—okay, barring Pittsburgh—for the last few weeks. I think we're good."

"Lenore, I'm calling your parents if you don't step down right now," Miss Barber grabbed the corded phone on her desk. "Promise me you won't go investigating the murder."

Lenore looked over at Cass who seemed really worried, the scowl on her face growing by the second. Miss Barber still had the phone in her hand and a finger on the dial button. Cass might be sensing something right now, so it was best to back off.

"Okay," Lenore sighed.

"We won't investigate," Cass joined in.

"Good," Miss Barber put the phone back. "You may leave."

Both girls complained about the whole ordeal through lunch. Who did Miss Barber think she is?

"My arm started hurting when she told us to stay away and didn't stop until she hung up the phone," Cass said, grabbing her peanut butter and jelly sandwich. "I don't think she's a suspect, but I feel like we need to keep going."

"Agreed, but where do we turn now? My mom's suspicious and disapproving of us investigating, too," Lenore stabbed her juice box a little hard.

"Should we even try to turn to the police and see if they'll help us investigate?"

"They might tell us to go away, or force us to tell them what we know without anything in return."

"That's true," Cass said. "But I don't think these feelings I'm getting are going to stop unless we solve this case. We need to do it for Mr. Benson's sake."

"Agreed," Lenore said. She took the mystery notebook out of her backpack. "Let's try jotting down some of your suspicions."

Chapter Fifteen

"Are you sure it's okay to do this?" Cass asked Lenore. "Won't we get in trouble?"

"I've done it millions of times. We'll be fine," Lenore insisted.

Both girls were sitting on Lenore's bedroom floor—their homework and text books sitting next to them, ignored. Lenore's new cat was sitting on the ground with them.

She picked up her family's mobile landline and punched in the number written on a piece of scrap paper. As the line rang, she turned on the speaker phone.

"Hello?" a man answered.

"Hi, Mr. Ted Benson, Jr! How are you doing?" Lenore asked.

"Who is this?" he responded.

"It's Lenore Hurley. My friend Cass and I discovered your dad's body, remember?"

"Hi," Cass said shyly into the phone.

"Oh. Hey," Ted Jr. said. "What is going on?"

"Well, we keep thinking about what happened to your dad, and we wanted to ask you some questions."

"Why?"

"Because we're going to solve your father's murder."

There was a snort and then some hard laughter for a minute on the other end of the line. They heard him take a deep breath.

"Go ahead," he said.

"Where were you the night of the murder?" Cass asked.

"Home, in Louisville."

"Do you have any hobbies?"

"Woodworking and fishing."

"Oh, like your dad!" Lenore said, hoping to irk him. "Any kids?"

"Two daughters, both are at University of Kentucky—before you ask where they were the night of the murder. My wife Evangeline was with me here the whole time. We cooked in and watched TV," he said.

"Would there be any clear motive for anyone to kill your father?" Cass asked.

"Well, he was an as—jerkward growing up," Ted Jr. changed his language to prevent hearing childish gasps. "But he didn't have any more kids to disappoint after Allison and I. Maybe he spent more time fishing than the people he made plans with?"

"So, you're saying someone would kill him because he spent so much more time at the lake than with them?" Cass asked for clarification.

"Yeah."

Lenore and Cass looked at each other. Cass wrote it down in their notebook, and she felt some pain while talking with their suspect.

Lenore took a deep breath before asking the next question.

"Ted, why do you hate your father so much?" she asked. "He was an old guy with no money. What he did to you was years ago. What are you holding on to?"

The line suddenly buzzed. The girls looked at the phone. Ted Jr. hung up. As the girls listened to the dial tone, Merlin—her cat's new name—jumped on Lenore's bed and began to rub his head against Cass' right hand.

"Well, that's a dead end," Cass said, writing in the notebook.

"Maybe," Lenore said. "Unless he's maybe in cahoots with someone else? Why else would he hang up after we asked him some simple questions? How do you feel about him?"

"I mean I felt a bit of a tightness in my throat, but nothing else. Let's give him a star for somewhat-suspect. Three stars being most-suspect."

"Okay," Lenore looked at Merlin, whose hair was flying off of him as Cass petted him. "Who else should we suspect?"

"There's your neighbors, and then maybe those two randos from his funeral. We can ask your neighbors about them."

"True," Lenore said. "Should we call them now?"

"Eh, I kinda need your help catching up with pre-algebra."

"Okay, but let's write down a reminder to reach out to the Starks and the Jepsens."

"Deal. But please keep Merlin off my math book while I work."

Chapter Sixteen

Lenore's neighbors seemed fond of playing phone tag, particularly a one-sided match of it. Every single time they called, they were met with an answering machine. By Saturday, Lenore and Cass were begging Mrs. Hurley to drive them to their neighbors' since there was no sidewalk connecting the houses out in the country.

"Why are you going over there?" Mrs. Hurley asked as she typed on the computer.

"Because…" Lenore started, but was unsure where the sentence was going. "It would be good to get some…"

"…Closure. From them. About what they're feeling," Cass said.

"Yeah," Lenore finished.

Mrs. Hurley stopped typing and stared at them.

"You're trying to solve the case, aren't you?" Cass and Lenore both stood up straighter.

"What?" Lenore asked.

"I'm not stupid, girls. I know you both like mysteries and adventures, and you think one has finally been handed to you on a gold plate," she continued. "What you're doing is dangerous and could get you killed."

"So, we can't stop at the Starks' this afternoon?" Lenore asked.

Mrs. Hurley got up from her computer chair and grabbed her car keys.

"Actually, I need to get my pie plate back from Alexandra, so this would be a good reason to go over there," she said. "But I'm just getting the plate, and then we're going."

Cass nervously swayed back and forth next to Lenore on the Starks' doorstep. Mrs. Hurley rang the doorbell. The stone porch with wooden columns could use a sweeping, but nothing screamed out of the ordinary for her. Alexandra Stark opened the door slowly.

"Why, Marie, it's nice to see you and the girls," she said. "Would you like some tea?"

"Do you have chai?" Lenore perked up.

The Stark's house felt like it was out of a period show with vintage lamps, flower print furniture, and stained, fading rose wallpaper. To distract from the walls, framed family photos covered most of them at three-and-a-half feet. Crochet blankets also covered the furniture with small knit pillows saying things like "home sweet home" and "God bless this mess." The old lamps barely gave light to the room.

Cass tried not to spill her chamomile tea held in a pink china teacup as her heart started pounding. Lenore mindlessly sipped her chai on the small couch next to Cass. Her mom sat up straight in a chair with a tall back.

"Oh, Marie, I'm sorry I didn't return it sooner," Alexandra started. "Your pie plate is currently drying in the drying rack. I'll get Eugene to get it."

She took a sip of her Oolong tea.

"But how are you doing?"

"I'm alright. The twins keep me busy along with Lenore's volleyball schedule, which will be over soon," Mrs. Hurley said.

"Oh that's right, you're a housewife. That's so sweet," Mrs. Stark said. "That's so nice."

"Oh no, I work remotely," Mrs. Hurley responded.

Lenore and Cass were zoning out, dying of boredom when Eugene Stark softly came down the stairs. The old man walked with a hum and stopped to get his own cup of tea from the kitchen before returning to the living room.

"Hello hello, everyone," he said to the room. "Can I get you girls anything?"

"I'm good," Cass offered. "How are you, sir?"

"Happy to have guests," Mr. Stark said. "It's always good to host people over."

"Actually Mr. Stark, can we ask you some questions?" Lenore said after taking another sip of tea.

"Sure," he smiled, gingerly sitting down in another tall-backed chair.

"I know we talked at the funeral for a bit, but how close were you with Mr. Benson?" Lenore asked, leaning forward on the sofa.

"We went to church with him and often invited him to sit with us," Mr. Stark said.

"That's right," Lenore said. "What was he like in church?"

"Usually quiet. Seemed to always pay attention to the sermon," Mr. Stark said. "We always invited him to the Sunday social afterwards, but it was rare he stuck around."

"Why do you think he didn't stick around?" Cass asked, setting her tea cup on the table.

"I don't know. He just always said he had plans, but thanked us for the invite," Mr. Stark said.

"What was he like at the socials when he did stay?" Cass asked.

"Friendly. He liked having a chocolate donut with coffee and always talked to us about his recent doings."

"Recent doings?"

"Like fishing trips, bargains at the furniture store, getting emails from his grandkids."

"Did you know anything about his family?" Lenore asked.

"He always told stories about his wife Margie who died a few years before he moved here. Always spoke highly of his kids but never said he went to visit them."

"Adds up." Lenore jotted in the mystery notebook.

"Do you know if he had other friends?" Cass asked.

"I think he was associated with the Jepsens and some others at church," he said.

Mrs. Hurley gave a small cough.

"Alexandra, could I get that plate?" she asked.

"Yes, dear," Alexandra put her cup down and stood up. Her mom followed Alexandra into the kitchen.

Both girls paused as Lenore finished writing her notes.

"Speaking of, are you girls religious in any way?" Mr. Stark asked. "Are you Christians?"

"Lutheran," Lenore said.

"Catholic," Cass said.

Quiet settled around the three of them.

"But, if you're inviting us to go to service with you tomorrow, we'd be more than happy to oblige," Lenore offered.

"Yeah," Cass joined in.

Mr. Stark broke into a wide smile and clasped his hands in excitement.

"That's great," he said.

"What's great?" Mrs. Hurley interrupted. She was back, her pie plate in hand.

"We're going to church with Mr. and Mrs. Stark tomorrow," Lenore said.

Chapter Seventeen

Church bells thundered the next morning at St. Mark's. Cass and Lenore stumbled up to the church, still half asleep from talking all night at their sleepover. Both put on their best smiles as they met the Starks at the entryway. The elderly couple ushered them to their pew near the middle of the church.

Cass and Lenore looked a little crazy staring at every church goer that passed, hoping to see some familiar faces. The Jepsens waved to them from the front when the organ started playing, and everyone stood up for the service. The girls awkwardly nodded as the congregation seemed to sing a hymn that wasn't in the pew books.

During the homily, Cass zoned out as her heart started racing. She started looking around, hoping to find some clues off people like Sherlock Holmes. She got distracted by a baby staring back at her from two pews ahead who reminded her of Lucy. The baby had equally blue eyes and a vacant smile. She looked at the baby's family, disregarding them as suspects. She then looked to the family's left and thought she saw someone from Mr. Benson's funeral.

A seventy-ish looking woman wearing a burgundy lace scarf

was looking forward, paying attention with her head held high. Her dark grey and white hair was pinned back into a bun.

Cass closed her eyes and tried to remember all of the funeral attendees. There was Ted Jr. and Allison, their respective spouses, and the four grandkids. Then the Starks and Jepsens, Detective Gomez, Miss Barber, and then she and Lenore.

But she also remembered seeing two other figures, but only for a few seconds when they first scanned the church. But this woman had to be it. She had an air of reverence about her and seemed like the type to attend funerals to pay her respects. She couldn't put her finger on it, but she knew she had to talk to the woman. This thought reverberated through her brain over and over.

Cass tapped on Lenore's shoulder and tried motioning to the mystery woman without raising suspicion. Lenore raised her eyebrows to ask who she was pointing to, but Mrs. Stark leaned over and asked if they were okay. Both nodded, then winked at each other. Lenore went back to zoning out, and Cass kept her eyes on the mystery woman.

She'd be darned if she couldn't meet the woman after church. Cass' heart kept pounding; she didn't even realize everyone had taken communion, came back to their seats, and were standing again for the end of the service. Time flies when zoning out in church. As everyone started singing "Amazing Grace," she felt a touch on her shoulder and jumped. It was Mr. Stark.

"Whoa there, didn't mean to scare you," Mr. Stark said. "Do you girls want donuts and orange juice?"

Chapter Eighteen

Cass and Lenore were looking over their shoulders as they picked up drinks from the juice table. The reception hall was buzzing, unlike at Mr. Benson's funeral reception last week. Cass told Lenore about her hunch, and both were on the lookout for the woman in burgundy lace. As soon as she picked up a tiny plastic cup of milk, Lenore elbowed her at the sight of the mystery woman settling down next to the Jepsens.

Cass then led a beeline to the mystery woman. She was unsure what to say and wished she would come up with a plan quickly. The woman was sitting down with an older man about her age who Cass did not remember.

"Excuse me, ma'am, is this seat taken?" Cass heard herself ask politely.

"No, please take them!" the woman said. "Who are you girls?"

"Cassandra Fairchild," she said awkwardly, reaching over the table to shake the woman's hand. "But most people call me Cass."

"Lenore Hurley," Lenore followed up.

"Lenore, that's an unusual name," the woman said.

"Thanks, my mom doesn't like it," Lenore answered. "What

are your names?"

"I'm Betty Green, and this is my husband Joe," she smiled as she gestured to him.

"And you know us," Sherri smiled, gesturing between herself and her husband.

The Starks eventually made their way to the table and sat down at the two seats between Lenore and Joe Green.

"There you are, girls. We tried to find you for a minute after getting our coffee," Mr. Stark said. "Joe, Betty, how are you?"

"We're good, happily surprised the youth decided to sit with us," Joe said. "What brings you girls here today?"

"Well, we just wanted to visit the church because, um, you know…" Cass struggled.

"We were actually invited by Mr. Stark here to attend this morning," Lenore jumped in. "I'm neighbors with the Starks, and Cass and I are always willing to try something new. You both look familiar, have we seen you before?"

"Well, we don't do much but church and bingo nights at the senior center," Betty said. "We've volunteered at the Salvation Army bell ringer campaign, as well. Joe also volunteers at the food bank."

"Okay." Lenore wasn't sure where to go with this. "Hey, were you guys at Edward Benson's funeral a few weeks ago?"

"We were not," Betty replied. "We try to get to know everyone here, but he didn't stick around after service. I read about his murder in the paper. So shameful, what happened."

"Yeah," Cass murmured, upset that her hunch got the wrong person. How could this happen? She swore she saw Betty weeks before at the church.

"You know who knew Ed Benson well? This guy," Joe said as he grabbed a fifty-year-old man's arm to stop him from walking past the table. "Trevor Gibbons. Hey, Trevor, why don't you stop for a second? These girls want to meet with you."

"Hello, everyone." Mr. Gibbons stopped next to the table and waved.

"This is Cassandra and Lenore, and they are curious about the regulars here," Joe said. "Girls, Trevor helps organize events at the church. He was probably at Ed's funeral a few weeks ago."

"You were?" Cass looked up surprised.

"Edward Benson?" Trevor took a seat next to Cass. "Yeah, I knew that guy. I helped arrange his funeral with his family. They were quite something."

"Yeah, we were at the funeral, too," Lenore said. "His son sure knew how to give a eulogy."

"There was family resentment there," Gibbons said. "Is there anything you want to know?"

"Did you know him well?" Lenore asked.

"I delivered meals to him once a week with the church," he said. "His cats almost always tried to escape the house, but he always invited me in. So, I made him the last stop on my route since I knew he lived alone. We'd chat for a bit on my visits."

"Did you guys do stuff together?" Cass asked.

"We played chess, and let me tell you, he was still sharp as a tack," he said. "He beat me most of the time. The guy liked talking about his family, his cats, fishing, and anything weather-related. Before he died, he told me he was taking dancing lessons."

"Yeah?" Lenore asked. "Can you think of any reason why he'd take dance class?"

"Not sure," Trevor said. "Maybe there was a woman? It seemed like he had this look in his eyes when he talked about dancing or his weekend plans. Why are you asking?"

"Just curious," Lenore said. "By the way, who was the other person at his funeral? Cass and I attended with our guidance counselor, the Starks, the Jepsens, that detective, and Mr. Benson's family, but who was the other person beside you? I'm just keeping a mental record."

"That would have been Marnie Woodson," Trevor looked around. "I think she just left, but she'll be back next weekend. She also helps with the Meals on Wheels program here, so that's how she also knew him. We felt bad that another in our parish died, and we always go to the church's funerals."

Trevor looked at the watch on his wrist.

"11:30 already?" he asked. "Time flies. She definitely has to be home now with her kids. Well, it was awfully nice meeting you two girls."

He got up and left the church hall. Lenore looked at the clock on the wall above the doorway to confirm when she saw her mom patiently standing there. She made eye contact with her mom who nodded back to signal time was up.

"Hey, it was nice meeting everyone, but my mom is here to pick up Cass and me," she said.

The two got up and met Mrs. Hurley at the exit. Her mom led the girls to the minivan.

"Sorry to keep you waiting, Mom," Lenore said as they walked through the parking lot.

"How was the service?" Mrs. Hurley said. "Pastor Ellis was confused why you weren't at our church this weekend."

"It was good," Lenore said, opening the minivan door for her and Cass. They got in and buckled up.

"How was investigating the murder?" Mrs. Hurley deadpanned as she turned the key to start the engine.

"How dare you accuse us of only going to church to catch a murderer!" Lenore replied. "Can't we just go because Mr. Stark invited us?"

"I heard you two whisper yesterday you were going to look for more suspects," Mrs. Hurley said. "For two budding private investigators, you're both terrible at the 'private' part."
The girls exchanged a look. Cass grabbed the mystery notebook out of her tote bag along with a pen and began writing.

"If it helps, Mrs. Hurley, we didn't take notes during the service," Cass said. "But it was a little weird at the reception hall."

"I think Mr. Benson was having an affair," Lenore announced. "We met this guy who said Mr. Benson had a twinkle in his eyes when he mentioned dancing and going out on weekends. But he doesn't seem to have had a girlfriend with him at church or at The Roast."

"Yeah, totally," Cass said. "I think that's a good theory. We haven't met anyone introducing herself as his lady friend, either."

"Girls, this is all speculation," Mrs. Hurley said. "You don't know Mr. Benson's business since you never talked to him."

"Well, we're doing our best, and we'll crack this case further," Lenore said.

"Don't!" Mrs. Hurley said. "Are you guys trying to find a murderer or just spreading gossip? Maybe he was keeping things to himself for a reason. Can't you just be normal middle schoolers for once and worry about what you're wearing to your school's dance next week?"

"*Mooooom*, think of it as we're helping him and his family find closure." Lenore said. "Think of us! We need closure! Cass couldn't sleep after we found his body! Also, I already know what I'm wearing, I told you it's my light wash jeans with that sparkly blue top with the cool butterfly sleeves and my high tops."

Mrs. Hurley stopped at a stop sign and looked back at Cass.

"Cass, are you doing okay? You seem tense."

"Yeah, I'm fine," Cass said, biting her lip and looking down at the notebook. "It just doesn't make sense. I'm looking at our notes, and I don't get it. Mr. Benson was conclusively a boring old man. The only interesting thing about him was his potential secret relationship. So, why would someone kill him?"

Mrs. Hurley looked forward again, sighing to herself. She could ground Lenore for all of this nonsense, but the last time she privately talked to Detective Gomez for an update, he said the police department was struggling with the case. They ruled out serial killers and it being premeditated. The girls were probably safe from physical danger, and they could let them wander the back woods again.

She also knew that even if Lenore was grounded and was told to never investigate, Cass would still probably try to solve the murder, and Lenore would try to help in some form of fashion. She tried talking to Cass' parents, but with their busy life and work schedules, they were proud just to stay on top of their daughter's cross-country schedule. And she did not condone telling other parents what to do.

Overall, it was emotionally easier to let her oldest child play detective with her best friend than have her inside, glued to technology, and having no social interactions in person. Mrs. Hurley pulled up to Cass' house and told her to take care as she got out of the vehicle.

Cass got home before the rest of her family who were probably post-church grocery shopping. She took out her house key and got in quickly so the Hurleys couldn't see her get upset. It was easy to conceal her feelings in the car with Lenore arguing with her mom.

She ran to her bedroom sobbing, feeling like an idiot. She crashed on her bed, tears first into the pillow. She couldn't believe her feelings kept telling her Betty was the suspect when she wasn't. She was so convinced. How could she be so wrong?

Immediately, Cass felt something soft rubbing up against her right arm and pawing at her face. It was Elroy, who must have been napping under her bed. She stopped sobbing as Elroy began kneading her quilt.

Cass then asked herself what Lenore would tell her at this very moment. She'd probably be nice and tell her if she didn't notice Betty Green, she wouldn't have met Joe Green. And if she hadn't met Joe Green, then she wouldn't have met Trevor Gibbons. And if she hadn't met Mr. Gibbons, then she wouldn't have valuable intel. Therefore the precognition wasn't wrong—it was simply being complex.

Cass pet Elroy to the sound of his lawn mower-esque humming. She felt herself calm down with each purr. Her tote bag was still around her right wrist, so she grabbed the mystery notebook and made sure everything was documented. She glanced at it, reviewing all of her thoughts. Between her bed's comfiness and the cat's purring, Cass quickly fell asleep.

Chapter Nineteen

Cass was running forward without a finish line to cross. Her trail started through the woods at Moon Town Middle School like it usually did—the trails twisting and her feet remembering the grooves of past jogs. She heard the school buses depart and the general sounds of students out for the day. She was reaching the end of the trail and could see only the back of her teammates, but then the forest pattern changed completely with the trails suddenly bending and the trees changing color to bright blue and pink from the usual fall pattern. They seemed to shimmer like she was in a fairytale, and she suddenly felt like she was no longer alone, hearing whispers as she passed them no matter how quickly she ran.

"You can't do it," an old voice whispered.

"You'll never make it," another said.

"It's hopeless," a third said.

Cass ran through a blinding light to the scene she wished she could block out. She was back on the same trail behind Lenore's house, running past Mr. Benson's body. It was totally silent except for the crunch of her shoes pounding the leaves. She wanted to keep running away, but the dream kept pushing her back to running near his body. She finally stopped, and it felt like the world slowed down.

Mr. Benson was still the pale, stiff-looking body that she remembered, but there seemed to be signs of life. Cass was standing over Mr. Benson when his crusty eyes opened. He was muttering something, but she couldn't hear him. She bent over and his arm reached up, grabbing her elbow. He softly whispered.

"—ep going."

"What was that?" she whispered.

"Don't stop," he said.

"Cass, are you okay?" a soft voice said.

She opened her eyes to find her mom sitting on the edge of her bed. Mrs. Fairchild was scratching Elroy's ears as he purred.

"What?" Cass asked, confused.

"I think you passed out after coming home from that service," Mrs. Fairchild smiled.

"I guess so," Cass yawned.

"So, how was it?"

"Um… it was good?" Cass tried remembering what happened that morning. "So, where is everyone else?"

"Your dad and Tommy are watching the football game, and Lucy is napping. Want to join us downstairs?"

"I have some homework to finish," Cass said.

"Well, come watch whenever you're done. I want to catch up," she said, then left her room.

Cass changed into some jeans and a t-shirt from her church clothes, then started her history homework as Elroy rubbed his head against her legs. Cass couldn't stop thinking about her dream, and took a break from learning about Bacon's Rebellion to write it down in her diary. She wasn't sure if she should include it in the mystery notebook, so she left that untouched. She decided to call Lenore for advice.

"I mean, do you remember anything different about Mr. Benson in the dream than when we saw his corpse in real life?" Lenore asked. "Other than him being alive, of course."

"Not really," Cass said. "He was like a less-creepy zombie."

"But I think it's encouraging he wants us to keep going," Lenore said. "Do you think he was speaking to you from beyond the grave?"

"I don't know. I'm not sure what that would look like."

"Me neither, but I figured it was worth asking you," Lenore paused for a moment before Cass heard her telling her dad she was on the phone. "Hey, I have to go now, but I'll see you tomorrow."

"Okay."

"I don't know what happened to you in the last few hours, but keep your head up. We must be doing something right. Bye!"

Cass hung up and breathed a sigh of relief. It wasn't only a scary dream. Maybe Lenore had a point. They had to keep going.

Chapter Twenty

Another day, another criminal put away for robbery and assault. Detective Gomez kept his poker face on as he left the Alleghany County courtroom, happy to see justice served to the victims of a drug store robbery eight months ago. He walked by the district attorney's office to say hi before heading back to Moon Town.

"Hey, Gomez," Assistant District Attorney Dominic Hurley stepped right up to him. "How are you feeling? Can we chat for a minute in my office?"

This was kind of surprising for the detective since they didn't talk a lot, but he followed his acquaintance to the office, anyway. It was decorated with law books and degrees, but also a little family-of-five portrait and drawings from his three kids on his desk. Two were badly drawn in crayon. The third drawing was an anime-esque picture of a girl holding a peace sign in one hand and a volleyball in the other, on college ruled paper. It immediately hit him what this was going to be about.

"Thank you, Detective," Mr. Hurley said, closing the door and sitting in his leather chair.

"No problem," David said. "You want to speak to me about your daughter and her friend investigating the Benson case?"

Mr. Hurley let out a big laugh.

"Yes, I should have known you'd pick up on that," he started. "Not just that, of course. The girls seem to have this lead where they think Mr. Benson had a secret lover. Something to do with what his church friends told them."

David's eyes widened at the news. It wasn't unheard of for old people to have affairs, but still.

"Okay, thanks," he said. He grabbed a tiny notebook out of his jacket. "Anything else?"

Chapter Twenty-One

Cass was exhausted as she opened her locker the next morning at school. She slowly turned the combination and opened the door, shoving her backpack inside.

"Guess what?!" someone said from behind her locker door.

"AH!" Cass jumped, shutting her locker to see her best friend. Lenore started laughing.

"Sorry!" she smiled. "You okay?"

"Just sleepy," Cass yawned. "What's up?"

"After we hung up, I looked up Marnie Woodson online, and it turns out she's in the same neighborhood as you! She's a few blocks away, but I got her phone number. So after dinner, I called her and asked if we could meet with her this week, and she said she's free this Thursday. We are going to meet her at 4:30."

Cass stared at her friend for a minute as her brain was still adjusting to the new day.

"Sorry, that's a lot to take in, but awesome!" Cass exclaimed. "I can't believe you were able to do that. Isn't your mom annoyed about all of this?"

"I think she's annoyed, but she said it's okay as long as we tell your mom about it and keep them informed about where we'll be."

"Okay, we'll save Marnie some room in the mystery notebook."

✳✳✳

Both girls couldn't wait to get through the week to meet with Marnie Woodson. Their respective sports seasons had wrapped up before Halloween, and they didn't have anything to look forward to after school now. The cross-country team named Cass the girls' MVP for the season, but that didn't magically solve all the jumpiness she now couldn't get out by running around after school. She would have to wait until track and field season in the spring and hope Coach Webber would bring back winter conditioning.

As she and Lenore started sifting through the millions of questions they wanted to ask Marnie, they worried she wouldn't have much to say about Mr. Benson. But they also didn't want to leave any clue unturned.

As their classmates asked what they would be wearing to the upcoming dance, Cass and Lenore were hoping for answers to more important questions. Lenore came to school Thursday dressed for the part—khakis, a light blue polo, and brown flats.

"You look like you attend private school," Cass lightly ribbed.

"I mean, she does work for a church. I think we shouldn't dress flashy," Lenore replied earnestly. "She might get insulted and not give us much."

"Think about it, no one at the church Sunday worried that you were wearing a red blouse with muddy boots."

"Hey, you told me they weren't noticeably muddy!"

"Yeah, because they weren't, and no one said anything to you about it. You're just making stuff up in your head about this woman because you're worried and overly prepared."

"And you aren't?"

Cass hurt a little at the retort. She could not sleep the night before, thinking about the interview along with her impending sense of doom keeping her up. This interview could blow the case open for them, and that had her on edge.

"I am, but not to the point where people think I write honor codes on top of my tests and quizzes," she went back to teasing.

Both girls stared at their classrooms' clocks all day. As soon as the final bell rang, they ran to the parking lot in search of Mrs. Fairchild's SUV. Cass' mom was a little startled when her daughter yanked the passenger door open quickly.

"Girls, you still have an hour and a half until you meet this woman, what's the rush?"

Cass and Lenore felt dumbfounded. Neither responded for a minute.

"Touché, Mrs. Fairchild," Lenore said. "Touché."

"By the way Lenore, you look very nice this afternoon," Mrs. Fairchild said. "Did you have a class presentation?"

"Is this outfit really off-putting for everyone?" Lenore asked, annoyed.

Ten minutes until the interview, Mrs. Fairchild put Lucy in a stroller and led the girls to Marnie's front door. She looked at them both.

"It's your interview," she told them. "I'll be back in fifteen minutes."

Lenore rang the doorbell as Cass took some deep breaths on the clean white porch with decorative pumpkins. Marnie opened the door slowly.

"Why, hello. You must be Lenore and Cass," she greeted them. "Come in."

The woman, in her fifties, led them from the foyer of her home to a white and blue living room. She had a quiet but friendly air about her. Maybe it was her slender build, the graying hairs interspersed with her short black hair, or the calm brown eyes. Maybe it was the eucalyptus wax melts she had scenting the house. The girls sat on a firm blue couch. Both requested tea when Ms. Woodson asked them if she could get them anything. After she came back out with the drinks, a little white and black Shih Tzu came running out and jumped up next to Lenore.

"Don't mind Zazu, he loves meeting new people," Marnie said.

Lenore petted the dog, and Cass took out the mystery notebook.

"Thanks for meeting with us, ma'am," Cass said.

"It's my pleasure," she said. "What can I help you girls with?"

"We noticed you were at Edward Benson's funeral and wanted to ask how you knew him," Lenore said.

"I met Ed years ago when he moved here from Danville," she said. "I was excited when he joined the church, and I told him about our volunteer activities. He volunteered once to usher people for our Christmas service, but that was it. I met with him a few times for our weekly meal service, and he was always pleasant."

"So, to be in the weekly meal service—can anyone at the church sign up?"

"No, it's more for old people, usually on government-assisted incomes, who can't travel out often or may be food insecure," Marnie said.

"Food insecure?" Cass asked.

"That's when people who aren't necessarily starving still struggle with hunger, paying their bills, and or don't know where their next meal is coming from."

"But we saw Mr. Benson every week at The Roast of Moon Town," Lenore said. "How could he not afford his meals but afford coffee once a week?"

"I don't know," Marnie said. "His financial decisions were his, but the parish council found he still qualified for the program. Maybe he was using the system, or maybe coffee in public was how he got through his loneliness. He told me he liked black coffee, and that's really not a pricey drink."

"That's a good point," Cass said. "Ms. Woodson, would you know by any chance if Mr. Benson had a girlfriend?"

"Excuse me?" she said, taken aback.

"Well, we found some jewelry in his house, and Trevor Gibbons said he would talk to the old man every week and he had a sneaking suspicion he was having a secret affair," Cass said. "Not like, in a bad way, but just that Mr. Benson seemed happy and was learning to dance."

"Oh, I didn't see him often near the end of his life," she said calmly.

"Okay, was there anything different about him you noticed at any point in the years you knew him?" Lenore asked.

"Not really," Marnie paused. "Well, there was this one time, I guess. Trevor was sick for the week, so I did his meal delivery routes a few years ago. After giving Ed his food, I asked him how he was doing. He at first gave a short reply, but then he changed tone after we were talking about the upcoming holidays. He said he was two hundred dollars short that month for a payment and asked if I could help. I told him I'd ask the church, and some of us scrounged together funds to give him. I later asked Trevor about it—if Ed said anything to him. Trevor said the old man thanked him and hugged him for a bit. I never heard about him asking for money since."

"Wow," Cass said.

"Now, I want to ask you two. What are all these questions for? What are you writing in that notebook?"

Cass felt her heartbeat start racing. She really hoped Marnie wasn't the murderer or going to hurt them.

"We're solving Mr. Benson's murder," Lenore said determined.

"Oh, how wonderful," Marnie smiled. "It's so terrible what happened to him, and I'm worried people aren't telling the police anything because they don't trust cops."

Marnie got up from her straight-back chair and stretched

before motioning the girls toward the front door.

"Well, thank you for coming, girls. In addition to the murder case, are you girls doing anything for fun?"

"Cass does cross-country and I play volleyball for Moon Town Middle, but our seasons just finished," Lenore said as she walked out the front door. "We have a dance tomorrow, I guess."

"Oh that sounds fun! Good luck," Marnie said, then shut the front door.

"Good luck with the case or the dance?" Cass said as she turned to Lenore.

Chapter Twenty-Two

"So if he was basically broke, why would he buy weekly coffee?" Lenore was thinking out loud.

"Like Marnie said, black coffee is, like, two dollars. It's not like he was buying double pump fraps," Cass replied. "Do you think he ever stopped and wondered when he would be sipping a grossly bitter drink for the last time ever?"

"As in, thinking of his natural ending or by murder? I don't know," Lenore answered her own question. "By the way, I called my other neighbors, the Jepsens, last night. They're free tomorrow afternoon and said they'd talk to us to help us."

"Okay," Cass said. "Even though these are the last people who attend the funeral, they're not the last suspects are they?"

"I mean, last suspects we probably know, but maybe they'll point us in the right direction. But Marnie was kind of short with us by the end. Trevor also seemed to want to get out of the conversation, too. Maybe just keep them as light suspects. Cass, your talents will definitely come in handy tomorrow."

Cass and Lenore kept going over the new information from Marnie, and were so into analysis, they didn't realize everyone else was staring at them. They leaned a foot away from the girls at the lunch table on Friday.

"Hey guys, can you stop talking about that dead guy?" Jada asked.

"Sorry," Lenore said. "What do you want us to talk about?"

"What are you guys wearing to the dance tonight?"

"Blue sparkle top and jeans," Lenore said. "My mom said she'd curl my hair a little."

"I have this green dress I figured I'd pair with a black belt and silver flats," Cass said. "What about you?"

"I figured it was nice jeans and cool hoodie night," Jada said. "I have this teal hoodie my mom bought me that's awesome and will go well with my heart necklace. I can't take off the hoodie since I'm wearing a spaghetti-strap tank top under it."

All the girls at the table nodded to the awkwardness of the dress code.

"So does anyone want to dance with certain crushes?" Emma Stanwell asked the table.

A few girls giggled. Jada blushed.

"Hopefully Lucas Matthews," she said. "I mean, he mentioned he was free for the dance, so I'm wishing he's still free."

"The guys in our class are duds," Lenore sighed.

"He's in eighth grade, isn't he?" Emma picked at Lenore. "Didn't you dance with Noah Thompson at the spring dance last year?"

Lenore turned bright red and didn't say anything.

"What about you, Cass?" Emma asked.

"Honestly, I haven't thought about it," Cass said. "So long as he uses deodorant by now and isn't gross."

The bell rang, and while all the girls left the table for their various classes, Cass was feeling pulled in two directions. She wanted to be excited for the dance, but she kept thinking about the murder case. Later that afternoon, she got ready for the dance at Lenore's house.

"I don't know about this dress anymore. You look really cool in those jeans, and I look too formal," Cass started babbling as Lenore's mother was curling her hair.

"Honey, you look great," Mrs. Hurley said.

"Yeah, that's a cute dress," Lenore said encouragingly, looking at her through the bathroom mirror. "Would you feel better if you dressed it down a bit? I have some silver leggings and green casual sneakers that might fit you."

Cass quickly opened Lenore's closet in search of her friend's suggestions. She found the green low tops, but Lenore's closet was all dresses or tops. No leggings.

"I can't find them," Cass yelled from her friend's bedroom.

"Bottom dresser drawer," Lenore yelled back.

Cass scrambled to the drawer and found the shiny leggings and changed into them. She felt a little better, but still plain weird. Why was she feeling this way about the dance? Was another mystery afoot?

She walked back to the family bathroom for approval.

"You look awesome," Lenore said as her mother finished her hair.

"You look great, Cass! Do you want me to do your hair, too?"

Cass nodded awkwardly. As Mrs. Hurley brushed her hair, she felt tension throughout the girl's neck and shoulders.

"Are you doing okay, Cass?"

"Yeah, I think so," Cass said. "I don't know why I feel so 'bleh' before this dance."

"Maybe you're nervous because you're so excited," Mrs. Hurley said. "Do you want to dance with anyone?"

"No, the only guys I know are my weird cross-country and track teammates, and then the dumb guys in our classes."

"Maybe you're just excited at the thought of it," Lenore said. "Last year, the now-eighth graders tried to block the doors and stop us poor sixth graders from attending. Now, they have to let us dance because we're no longer at the bottom of the food chain."

"Didn't you dance with a seventh grader last year?" Mrs. Hurley asked.

"Yeah, and?"

Mrs. Hurley finished giving Cass a messy braided bun. Cass checked herself out in the mirror and gave a little smile to her new casual look.

"Thanks, Mrs. Hurley," she said.

The girls rushed to the minivan, anxious to get to the action. Mrs. Hurley pulled up to the front of the school.

"You girls have fun! No murder investigating tonight!"

Lenore jumped out of the car without looking back, but Cass felt confused at the comment. How could Mrs. Hurley read her mind like that? She didn't want to think about Mr. Benson's death, but it seemed to stick around in her head like an echo.

As they walked into the gym, Cass felt her heart matching the beat of the loudspeaker's music blasting. The school's cafeteria had been transformed to reflect the fall season with paper maple trees, a giant full moon at one end of the room, and the rented disco ball rotating from the ceiling. She looked around for others with Lenore when her best friend walked up to her group of volleyball friends. Cass knew some of them but wasn't very close with them. She went up to her cross-country friends, instead, and talked with them.

It took some songs to get the awkward students to the middle of the dance floor when a line dance song began playing. Suddenly, the space flooded with seventh and eighth grade classes mostly trying their best to be in rhythm. More students stayed on the dance floor after the song; Cass and Lenore got lost in the music, dancing and singing loudly until a slow song came on. Cass looked around for a guy to dance with. Lenore loudly announced she was going to the bathroom for the song.

A few seconds later, Cass felt a tap on the shoulder. Class goofball Connor Flemming stood in front of her, wearing a striped orange and blue polo.

"Hey, have you seen Lenore?" he shouted over the music.

"Bathroom!" Cass replied.

"Oh…" an awkward silence hung around them before he

spoke again.

"Well, do you want to dance?"

"Sure," Cass said, still speaking loudly to be heard over the blaring music.

She wasn't sure what to do, so she put her hands on his shoulders as he grabbed her waist. They swayed to the music. Cass wasn't sure whether to look at Connor or around the room. She tried looking at him as he gave an awkward smile at her. She suddenly noticed he strongly smelled of brand store body wash her dad used. She laughed awkwardly.

"I'm sorry. I don't know how to do this," she announced.

"It's okay," Connor said. "Just look at me for at least thirty seconds."

"Okay!" she shouted.

"You can breathe," he said.

Cass gasped for breath, realizing she had been holding it.

"Sorry."

"It's okay. Just be present for the song and your partner."

"Hey Connor, if you're constantly getting in trouble, why do you know all this stuff about dance etiquette?"

"My dad made me learn a few years ago when my older siblings were all getting married."

They were both silent for a few seconds, but Cass did feel better. The eighties ballad ended, and Connor waved to Cass as he left to join his friends. Lenore was immediately back by her side.

"What was that?" Cass asked.

"I just had to go to the bathroom?"

"The whole song?"

"Yeah, why?"

Both rejoined the group of friends they were with and continued to have fun. For a minute, Cass completely forgot the case she and Lenore were working on. She didn't have a single worry on the brain and was happy to shake off her extra energy while dancing. After a few songs, she and Lenore headed over to the snack table to take a break.

Cass was snacking on tortilla chips when she suddenly laid her eyes on him from ten feet away. The boy was slightly gangly with jet black hair and dark brown eyes. His skin was light brown and his light blue polo complimented it with his smile perfectly. She couldn't stop staring at him as he laughed with his friends while holding a plastic cup full of soda.

"EARTH TO CASS! You there, girlie? Hey! You're getting chips on your dress," Lenore yelled as she waved her left hand in front of her friend, snapping Cass back into reality.

"What?" Cass wiped crumbs off her dress. "Is my face okay?"

"Yeah!"

"Is mine?"

"Yeah, I just said so," Lenore said. "Are you having a stroke?"

To both girls' shock and excitement, a second slow song began playing. Lenore disappeared again, and Cass wasn't sure what to do. She looked down at Lenore's green low-tops she was wearing when she heard, "Hey! Want to dance?" It was the boy she had been staring at.

"Sure!"

"I don't think I know you! What's your name?" he asked as he put his hands on her waist.

"I'm Cass Fairchild. I'm a seventh grader, if that helps."

If that helps? Cass felt very stupid as she forced herself to make eye contact with those dark brown eyes.

"Actually, it does," he said. "I'm Leo Fernandez! I'm an eighth grader, but I swear I didn't try to bar you guys from dancing last year."

"It's okay. I don't remember that dance as the epitome of my year, anyway."

"So, Cass. What do you like to do?"

"I'm on the cross-country and track and field team here. I actually just got MVP for the girls."

"Oh, cool!"

"Yeah, I like reading and solving mysteries."

"Mysteries?"

"Yeah!" She couldn't believe she spouted the next few sentences. "Like, you remember hearing about the dead guy found in the woods a month ago? My best friend and I discovered the body, and now we're trying to solve the mystery."

"No way! Are you going to get in trouble?"

"Maybe with my best friend's mom, but nothing bad so far."

"That's cool!"

"What do you do for fun?"

"I'm in the engineering club and the baseball team."

"Cool!"

There was a comfortable silence for the next thirty seconds that made Cass feel calm until the song ended. Leo thanked her and went back to his friends. Cass felt every emotion at the same time and ran to the bathroom.

"Lenore?" she croaked.

"Cass?" Katie Crombie asked as she walked out of a stall and to the sink to wash her hands.

"Oh, hey," Cass said a little too casually. "Have you seen Lenore?"

"No, but I saw you with Leo Fernandez. Gonna ask him out for Valentine's?" she teased.

Cass awkwardly laughed and slipped out of the bathroom. She found Lenore casually hanging out by the water fountain.

"LENORE! Where were you?"

"I was going to say the same to you. After I danced with Noah, I couldn't find you."

They went back to the dance floor and the next hour melted away. The paid DJ ignored everyone's groans as they played the last song of the night, a slow country ballad. Lenore looked for Noah Thompson like an activated sleeper spy, and Cass was left to fend for herself. She ended up bumping into classmate Adain Peters and danced with him. As soon as the last song ended, the lights immediately went back on. Cass and Lenore reconnected at a table where they left their purses.

"Your mom is parked out by the front," Cass said as she put

down her phone.

"Okay," Lenore said, turning toward the exit. Cass followed her friend. She eyed Leo loitering with his friends by the door. She tried to wave when he said, "See ya, Cass."

"Bye Leo!" her voice accidentally squeaked.

"You're turning red," Lenore whispered to her.

"No I'm not," Cass further squealed.

"Yes, you are! Did you just meet him?"

"Yeah, when you ran off for Noah during the second slow song."

Lenore rolled her eyes. They found Mrs. Hurley's minivan and got in the middle row.

"How was the dance, girls?"

"Good. Cass met an eighth grader."

"Shut up," Cass put both of her hands to her face.

Chapter Twenty-Three

"So do you think you'll try and find Leo Fernandez on Monday?" Lenore asked Cass, lying on her sleeping bag in the Hurley den. The lights were out and both girls' dance highs were starting to wear off.

"Depends," Cass said from her sleeping bag on the couch. "Will you, if you find out Noah Thompson is single?"

Lenore gasped.

"First off, Stacey Kinsley said she was dating him last spring! I didn't know he was single the whole year until he told me a few hours ago," Lenore said matter of factly. "Second, it's not embarrassing to have a crush! Leo is a cute guy, and you'd have time to date him before he graduates and goes to high school."

"Still," Cass said. "It was just a dance."

"I've never seen you turn that red before, not even when you got caught passing me a note in Mrs. Leary's class and had to read it out loud."

"He was really, really cute," Cass admitted. "But what if I find out he does something I don't like or realize he's toxic."

"Dump him and move on."

"True," Cass said. "It was funny, seeing him made my heart

race a million miles per minute, so at first I thought it was related to the case. But then when I danced with him, it was like I forgot about poor Mr. Benson."

"We still have tomorrow to talk to the Jepsens," Lenore said. "We don't need to dwell on it right now. Maybe when we wake up."

Both soon fell asleep. The next day Cass woke up to the smell of Mr. Hurley's signature blueberry pancakes. Lenore was already in the dining room kitchen, looking at the mystery notebook as she sipped on herbal tea.

"Good morning, Miss Cassanda," Mr. Hurley offered. "Pancake?"

"Yes, please," Cass yawned. "Morning Lenore."

"Morning," Lenore closed the notebook. "I think the Jepsens will be easy to talk to today with our new leads. Ask them about a potential affair and if Mr. Benson was in debt. We can write down our questions after breakfa—"

"After homework," Mr. Hurley interrupted as he plated Cass' breakfast.

Lenore rolled her eyes.

"After homework, we can write down our questions or improvise, depending on how you're feeling."

"I'm feeling like I have room for some bacon," Cass hinted to Mr. Hurley. He returned to the oven where it was cooking.

"This is so exciting, first we have a dance, now we have new leads," Lenore said. "It's going to be a good weekend."

"A good weekend also concentrating on your homework," Mr. Hurley jumped in. "Eleanor Rose, you agreed with your mother and me that this week homework and school come before solving mysteries."

"Fine," Lenore said.

Mr. Hurley finished plating the bacon and cleaning up the dishes before leaving the room. He told them to call for him once they finished school assignments and went back to his office. Cass and Lenore sighed through the hour and a half spent on class assignments, occasionally looking at the clock. The interview wasn't until midafternoon, but the wait was excruciating.

Cass and Lenore marched from the kitchen table to the living room where Mr. Hurley was watching college football. He didn't seem interested in either team playing and muted the volume when the girls approached him.

"All done?" he asked.

"Yep," Lenore replied.

"Well, let's get to the interview," he stood up.

"Dad, the interview isn't until two, we have a few hours on our hands," Lenore replied.

"Oh, want to take a walk then?"

Cass and Lenore shrugged at each other before nodding. More leaves were piling up in the woods as Cass and Lenore stepped into the trees with Mr. Hurley. He wasn't sure where to lead them. He took a left at the fork where the girls usually went right.

Cass and Lenore snickered at each other as Mr. Hurley walked ahead of them. He didn't know what he was doing, but kept telling them which path to take whenever it split. Cass wondered how Lenore could be his kid with his lack of directional skills. Whether on purpose or by mistake, he led them to the back of Mr. Benson's house. There was still some police tape on the trees where his body had been found.

"Well, this isn't right," he said. "Girls, are you okay?"

"Yes, Dad. Mr. Benson wasn't killed in his house," Lenore said.

"What do you mean he wasn't killed in his house?"

"We went through his house already with his kids. All of the kitchen knives were there with the other utensils. All the big knives were in the cutting block, plus there's no sign of a forceful entrance or exit, nor any blood anywhere. Dad, his blood was all over the leaves where we found him, but there wasn't any here, and his body was wrecked by the weather from the night before."

Mr. Hurley stared at his daughter, shocked she knew so much

about crime scene investigation. He looked at his watch, unsure what else to do.

"Okay, Moon Town CSI, are you ready to turn around for maybe a light lunch?"

"Sure, when Cass returns."

"Wait, where is Cass?"

"Right here," Cass called from the left side of the house. "I just did a light perimeter search and saw a for sale sign on the house. Also, if you're offering, I'd like some mac and cheese when we get back, sir."

Back at the house, the girls talked about Mr. Benson's house as they finished their lunch.

"Hey, Dad, does the realtor have to tell clients if the house they're selling used to belong to a murder victim," Lenore asked her lawyer dad.

"No, sellers aren't required to disclose death on the property they're selling."

"Why?"

"Boring Pennsylvania Supreme Court stuff. Now, are you girls ready to visit the Jepsens?"

They put their mac and cheese bowls in the kitchen sink.

The Jepsen's doorbell wasn't working, so Lenore pounded the ornate chimp door knocker. Mrs. Jepsen answered the door after a second.

"Sorry, girls, we just put down our baby for a nap, if you could be a little more quiet," she said.

"Baby?" Lenore asked. The Jepsens were in their late seventies and had children far away whom they never mentioned before.

"Maury, our Macaw was up all night; he needs a midafternoon nap," she offered.

"I know a thing or two about children who don't sleep," Mr. Hurley let himself in the house after the girls. He shook Mrs. Jepsen's hand as they walked through the front door.

The Jepsen's house was dark but also surprisingly

comforting. The maroon wallpaper complimented the worn down off-white couch, sitting chairs, and light brown tables. The dark brown curtains made it hard to tell what time of day it was.

No wonder the bird had a hard time telling day and night, Cass thought to herself.

Cass and Lenore sat on the eggshell-colored love seat together. Mr. Hurley sat in a wooden chair near the small TV. Mrs. Jepsen walked into the kitchen through flipping doors and returned with a tray full of shortbread cookies and tea.

"Make yourselves at home," Mrs. Jepsen offered. "Lenore, I heard you love chai, so I got some apple spiced chai, and Cass, Alexandra said you liked the store brand honey vanilla chamomile."

She placed the tray in front of them and they all said their thanks. Cass was surprised but delighted at the warm reception.

Sherri's husband John entered the room and sat in a small white seat. Mrs. Jepsen took the wooden rocking chair.

"So, we just had a few questions to ask, if you don't mind," Lenore started. Cass grabbed the mystery notebook out of her bag.

"Go ahead," Mrs. Jepsen said.

"So, on the night Mr. Benson was killed, where were you guys, and did you hear anything?"

The elderly couple exchanged glances before John spoke.

"We were here just cooking and having a night in," John said. "We heard some animals outside, the usual squirrels or foxes passing on the leaves, but nothing that alerted us to a crime."

"How well did you guys know him?" Cass asked.

"We went to church with—" John started.

"But he sat by himself mostly and rarely went to Sunday social," Lenore interrupted. Everyone was silent for a few seconds. "Sorry, we've heard that line a lot before. I didn't mean to interrupt. Go on, please."

"Well, we didn't know much about his churchgoing because we left as soon as he did," John said.

"Did you just go straight home like him?" Cass asked.

"Usually John drops me off so he can go volunteer at the supermarket as a greeter and get us groceries," Mrs. Jepsen said. "I stay here and garden and clean."

"But sometimes he would come over on Sunday evenings with fish he caught and beer to chat with us."

"Oh?" Cass said. "What did you talk about?"

"Mostly just me and Edward," John spoke up. "We'd drink while Sherri cooked up dinner. Then the three of us would have a nice meal. He'd leave soon after that."

"What did you talk about?" Lenore asked.

"He would just bring up stories of his home life and kids," he said.

"Did he bring up any enemies or someone he doesn't like?" Lenore asked.

"No, he was in his seventies," John said. "His enemies may have been Louisville and Duke's basketball teams."

Cass and Lenore paused. The former felt like they were skipping over Sherri's days with Edward.

"So, going back a bit, Mrs. Jepsen," Cass said. "Do you have any favorite flowers in the garden? Did Mr. Benson ever ask for flowers for anything while he was over?"

"I have some rose bushes, and no," Mrs. Jepsen said. "Why would he ask for flowers?"

"Well, why wouldn't he? Secret girlfriend?" Cass suggested.

Both of the Jepsens laughed.

"Oh dear, who would want to date that old man?" Mrs. Jepsen said.

"We don't know, but it could be possible," Lenore said. "You never really know someone until they reveal themselves to you."

"That was very wise," Mrs. Jepsen said.

"Thanks. My mom said it first," Lenore replied.

"I guess we just don't know about him," Mrs. Jepsen continued.

"But he had ruby earrings and some makeup left at his place," Cass offered. "And we're doubting he likes costumes."

Mrs. Jepsen's eyes gleamed at Cass' comment.

"Jewelry?" she said. "Do you have it on you so I can see it?"

"No," Lenore asserted.

"Oh."

"But it was some ruby earrings and a gold bracelet we found," Cass offered.

Mrs. Jepsen paused for a few seconds.

"I might have to think if anyone at church wears those," she said.

"Awesome!" Lenore cheered.

Right then, some loud squawking came from upstairs.

"That must be Maury," John got up. "Want to help, Dominic?"

"Uh, sure," Mr. Hurley got up and followed John out of the room.

Mrs. Jepsen rolled her eyes as the men left the room.

"I wanted a cat or small dog, but John is allergic to pet dander," she admitted.

"Oh," Lenore said. "My parents were anti-pet, but they had to let me take one of Mr. Benson's cats since his kids were going to dump them in the shelter. Merlin is much happier."

"Merlin?" Mrs. Jepsen asked. "He told us his cats were Murphy and Elroy."

"I renamed him from Murphy but he hasn't recognized it yet," Lenore sheepishly offered.

"So, have you renamed Elroy to 'Arthur,' Cass?" Mrs. Jepsen joked. "I assume you took him if Lenore has the one."

"Yeah, but he's still Elroy," Cass said.

"Hey, what if we rename our cats like 'Sherlock' and 'John'," Lenore pipped up. "Or 'Poirot' and 'Marple.'"

"Are you referring to Ms. Marple the spinster?" Mrs. Jepsen asked.

"Yeah! Okay, I see where you're going, the cats are both male…" Lenore left off.

"You seem to really like mysteries," Mrs. Jepsen said.

"Of course I do!" Lenore smiled. "They make life more interesting!"

"So, are you trying to solve this case because you're bored?"

Lenore was caught off guard. She leaned back a little on the couch.

"Oh, no!" Lenore went. "I'm sorry! I'm doing this for justice for Mr. Benson. Isn't that right, Cass?"

"Yeah," Cass said as she sipped her tea.

Lenore took another bite of the shortbread cookie and then her stomach rumbled.

"Hey, where's the bathroom?" She stood up.

Mrs. Jepsen stood up, as well. "Just down the hall and the first door to the left. Please spray with the air freshener when you're done."

Lenore left the room as the two watched her go. Mrs. Jepsen sat back down, and Cass looked at her for a few seconds as she looked back. An awkward silence started to fill the room.

"You seem to know Mr. Benson better than others here," Cass offered. "Do you miss him?"

"He was a bit of an odd bird, but I do," Mrs. Jepsen said. "I felt kind of bad for him. He was married for forty years and then suddenly widowed. Everyone else here has been with their husbands and wives for as long, and still going. John and I just celebrated fifty-two years recently, ourselves. I don't know what I'd do without him. We do everything together. Everything."

Cass' right foot tapped against her left.

"You okay, Cass?" Mrs. Jepsen said.

"Yeah," Cass said, fighting the urge to crack her knuckles. "Just fidgeting."

"How do you think your investigation is going?"

"Um, it's okay. We are trying to find more evidence and, well, suspects too," she said.

"Is that why you're fidgeting?"

"I don't know," Cass looked down.

"You can tell me," Mrs. Jepsen smiled.

"I just—I've been having dreams lately about Mr. Benson," Cass let out.

"Yeah, what happens in the dreams?"

"He's lying under the leaves, and he's telling me to solve the case," she said.

"Wow, and that's making you shake?"

Cass paused for a second, wondering if she should tell Mrs. Jepsen. She seemed really supportive so far. Might as well let her know cautiously.

"It's more of a sixth sense with the fidgeting. Like, I sense things before others perceive them," Cass said. "It helped me find the jewelry in Mr. Benson's house."

"Oh my," Mrs. Jepsen said. "Maybe it's making you more perceptive."

"Please don't tell anyone about this," Cass pleaded. "I wish it would all stop."

"Your secret is safe with me," she said, putting her fingers to her lips.

"Hey, if you leave church as soon as it's over, why were you there for donuts the other day?" Cass asked.

"We were just checking in on everyone," Mrs. Jepsen said. "Also, there's not much to garden this time of year."

The two of them heard Lenore talking then as she came back into the front room.

"Hey, Mrs. Jepsen, why do some of your floorboards squeak but others don't?" Lenore re-entered the room.

Mrs. Jepsen laughed softly.

"You'll like this, Miss Detective, we have false floorboards in this house! The houses in this neighborhood all have them."

She got up from her spot and walked to the center of the room.

"Can one of you girls lift this for me? My knees aren't as young as yours."

Lenore got up and walked to the spot Mrs. Jepsen was pointing at. She kneeled and fiddled with the false floor for about thirty seconds before opening it. The three of them looked at the soft pink slippers and a hummingbird feeder hidden below.

"Now I know what John is getting me for Christmas," Sherri laughed. "I know which room he'll hide my Valentine's Day gift in then."

Cass and Lenore looked at each other.

"Wait, if you have false floors, does that mean my house has false floors?" Lenore pondered out loud. "Would my parents hide my gifts there? Or maybe Jeanine and Jennie's?"

"Bigger picture, Lenore! Do you think Mr. Benson has false floors?" Cass nudged her.

"Oh, yeah! But, how do we get back in?" Lenore asked.

"I believe there's an open house starting at one o'clock tomorrow," Mrs. Jepsen offered. "John and I could come with some friends if you need any support."

Cass and Lenore's eyes grew big.

"Would you?" Lenore asked.

"Thank you!" Cass replied.

Mr. Jepsen and Lenore's dad then came downstairs to the living room. The girls quickly put the floorboard back in place and all three sat down to pretend they weren't spoiling Christmas morning.

"And that's why we have naps for our bird," John was concluding his story as the men walked back in.

"That's interesting," Mr. Hurley feigned interest before turning to the girls. "Are you both finished here?"

"Yes," Lenore started. "And guess what?"

"What?" her dad asked.

"We're going to Mr. Benson's house's open house tomorrow with the Jepsens to find more clues."

"After you finish homework, young lady."

"Ugh!"

Chapter Twenty-Four

Cass stared out of her window that evening as she looked through the mystery notebook. Mr. and Mrs. Jepsen were crossed out as suspects which left them back at square one. Cass had felt awkward around Mrs. Jepsen, but those precog feelings seemed to melt away the more she got to know her. She recognized how painfully shy she could be around adults.

Well, at least an adult is finally in our corner with the investigation, Cass thought to herself. *And they gave us further leads.*

Cass pulled out a plastic sandwich baggie from her dresser. It contained the earrings and the bracelet. Maybe Mrs. Jepsen knew who the jewelry belonged to?

Cass wondered if the rubies were real and looked up how to tell if the stones were fake. She took a dime to one of the earrings and scratched it. She learned in last year's science class that diamonds and jewels don't scratch. Time to put that to the test. She pulled the dime's ridge from the surface and it was plain as ever.

Huh, Cass thought.

✳✳✳

The next afternoon, the girls met up with the Jepsens outside the empty home. They kept on their church clothes to blend in with everyone going through the open house. They waved to the Greens who were also looking around. After some greetings, they all met the realtor Jan Schuur who pointed them toward snacks and orange soda in the parlor.

"Parlor?" Lenore turned to Cass as they found the area that used to have Mr. Benson's television, arm chairs, and cat photos. There was some plaster covering where the nails used to be, and the carpet was now a pale blue color—clean enough to eat brownies off it.

Some young couples mixed and mingled around the downstairs floor.

"Good luck searching, girlies, we'll distract anyone if we need to for you," Mrs. Jepsen winked.

"So, what should we do?" Cass asked Lenore.

"Maybe check the rooms when they're empty?"

"Okay, so go when no one is staring us down like Ms. Schuur right now?"

Both smiled politely to the realtor who smiled back, then began talking to a couple who appeared to be in their forties about tearing out carpeting and repainting a few rooms. They walked upstairs, carefully feeling for loose boards below them. Some guests stared impatiently at them as they walked slowly up the stairs. Between awkwardly passing strangers and trying to look normal, the girls were eventually reprieved when most of the prospective owners went downstairs. Lenore felt a squeak under her right foot in the upstairs hall.

"I think I found a loose one," Lenore said excitedly. She bent down and started picking up a loose floor panel. Cass helped her lift it up. They both reached their hands in the space eager for some final evidence as they blindly grabbed at items.

"This could be it," Cass smiled as she grabbed a fistful of items from the space. She was immediately disappointed when she noticed she was holding two packs of cigarettes and little bottles of vodka.

"What the heck?" she asked.

Lenore looked at her hands and realized she was holding yellow letters with small neat handwriting.

"We all have secret habits, I guess," Lenore said. "I wonder who wrote these?"

Cass' heart started racing. What was she going to do with these non-minor friendly items she was holding in her hands? What if she got caught? Why would Mr. Benson hide these if he lived alone?

You're getting in trouble, you're getting in trouble, you're getting in trouble, dashed through her head on loop as she stared at the items in her hands.

As she started sinking into the doom and gloom, Lenore's hand on her shoulder brought her back to reality.

"Hey, maybe we should put the plank back and go somewhere else before we're caught," she suggested. Cass nodded.

The girls moved to the empty guest bedroom and sat on the floor, ready to read the letters. They sat in the corner closest to the window light. Cass' hands were trembling, so Lenore kept the letters and read them softly. The author's handwriting was small and neat and consistently used dark blue ink.

"My dearest Coffee Bean,

It has been a few weeks since I've seen you. My flowers are blooming more and more each day. I'll make sure to cut some for you to keep at your house the next time I'm there. It's been too long.

Being sick has been unpleasant, but I'm thankful for all the support I've received. The community has been really caring. Thank you for chipping in for the experimental treatment, it's like

I've been brought back to life since I met you. Even before I was ill, you were like a medicine to the mundaneness of my life.
Until our next Sunday when we're holding hands, I'll cherish the thought of you. Can't wait to hold your hands as we dance.
Love,
Your Ruby
P.S. (Give the boys some forehead kisses for me)."

"'Your Ruby?' What kind of nickname is that," Lenore asked.
"Get it?" Cass exclaimed. "I found those ruby jewelry pieces in the bathroom. It's a codename!"
"Oh, that's good!" Lenore tried looking for a date on the letters but was stunned to find the page corners blank. Both were puzzled that the letters didn't have their envelopes even after rechecking the floor board.
"I wonder who the boys are?" Cass asked.
"Probably his cats," Lenore replied. "Let's try looking through these other letters."
The next one went into a lot of detail about their kissing, and Cass and Lenore really wished they hadn't read it. Cass wasn't sure if the running thought *"you're gross"* was directed at her or the letter writer, but she felt bothered by it all. Nervously, she asked Lenore to read the last letter in her hand. The next one was as intriguing as the first.
"My dearest Coffee Bean,
I had a lot of fun last weekend. I was always told vodka was such a vice for a person, and I probably shouldn't drink with my treatment, but I now think it was rather good when taken on the rocks. You have quite the taste.
I know it's hard splitting your time with the dud. But I promise, as soon as the mortgage is paid off (soon!) and my grandchildren are all married, I will leave him to be with you. I've never met someone as intellectually stimulating as you. You never know when love will find you, and I think I found it in someone true.

I know it's a long wait, but it's worth it. You are worth it all. I can't wait to dance with you when I'm completely recovered.
Send my love to Elroy and Murphy. I hope the boys are well and taking my departure fine enough. I know they miss me when they run up to me at every visit.
When I see you again,
Your Ruby"

"Whoa," Cass said, noticing the stairs creaking.

"So, we were right about the affair," Lenore said. "But we still have less of an identity. How is your precog feeling?"

"Without my precog, this is someone who was free on weekends," Cass said. "Second, my heart is just telling me this has to be the secret mistress. It also adds to Ms. Woodson's tale about him needing money all of a sudden. He wasn't just super poor, he was trying to help someone else."

Right away, Jan Schurr walked in the room. Cass quickly threw the cigarettes and vodka in her tote bag.

"So, what's going on here?" the realtor asked.

"Just chilling," Lenore said, tucking the letters in her purse.

"Oh, well, you're missing it right now, but a certain celebrity you girls may know just walked into the house."

"Ava Flynn?" Lenore asked.

"Nico McHale?" Cass asked.

"No, he's this indie musician called Kevin Scarpin—"

Lenore let out a small shriek.

"No way!"

"Um, yes. He's downstairs if you want to meet him," Schuur said, confused at the excitement.

"I have his EP! And his CDs! And a concert tee from last year! *ohmygoshicantbelievehesherewhatintheheckisgoingonamidreaming?*" Lenore screamed.

"What?" Jan asked.

Lenore got up from the floor and hurried downstairs. Cass and the realtor looked at each other.

"Are you also a fan?" Jan asked. "He apparently wanted to look at real estate near his hometown to feel grounded and saw the open house. Want to join your friend?"

"I'm not really into indie music like Lenore," Cass said. "But I should go check on her so she doesn't get her first restraining order at twelve-and-a-half years old."

Cass slowly walked down the stairs. She enjoyed going to Scarpino's Pittsburgh concert last year and remembered him saying something about living in the area. But she was annoyed at the second distraction this weekend from their investigation. There could be more floorboards in the house with secret love letters or insights. They also never checked out the unfinished basement.

Cass walked into the kitchen where she saw Mrs. Jepsen and Mrs. Green standing at the island. She joined them and watched her best friend fangirl.

"Are you a big fan of this young man, too?" Mrs. Jepsen asked.

"His music is pretty cool," Cass said.

"It seems like you're more invested in this case for Mr. Benson than her," Mrs. Jepsen said.

"Yeah, I guess," Cass said. "But this guy is Lenore's celebrity crush."

"I wouldn't put it past you that she might obsess about this now over the murder?"

"Maybe," Cass started disassociating.

She fished around her tote bag for the sandwich baggie.

"By the way, Mrs. Jepsen, here's the jewelry I found here before."

Mrs. Jepsen snatched the bag, and the old ladies looked at its contents.

"These are beautiful," Mrs. Green exclaimed.

"Truly radiant," Mrs. Jepsen said. "Ed must have really loved whoever this was for."

"Sure," Cass shrugged.

"Not all illicit affairs include something gorgeous like this," Mrs. Green said.

"You really like this," Mrs. Jepsen said.

"Who doesn't love a natural ruby?" Mrs. Green replied as she held the bag.

"Did you find anything in those floorboards?" Mrs. Jepsen asked.

Cass remembered she had the vodka and cigarettes on her, as well, and did her best not to blush.

"Nope," she lied. "They were empty like the rooms here."

"Oh," Mrs. Jepsen was surprised. "I would have figured he had something in there."

"Men always have something to hide," Mrs. Green said.

"I just didn't feel anything up there," Cass shrugged.

"Hopefully then those nightmares stop and you can go back to feeling normal," Mrs. Jepsen said.

"Yeah," Cass said.

Cass started dozing when Kevin Scarpino approached her. "You must be this fan's friend who also saw my show last year. Do you want to get a picture?"

Cass felt herself sour. The tall bleach blonde singer was dressed surprisingly more casually than his rock attire with guyliner—he was in a brown cardigan and corduroy pants. Cass put on a smile and agreed. She pulled out her smartphone since Lenore would want evidence she had met her celebrity crush.

After a few selfies and napkin autographs with the budding artist, the girls were taken home by the Jepsens.

Lenore freaked out in her bedroom as Cass sat on her bed, petting the cat.

"Oh my gosh! I danced with my crush this weekend and met Kevin Scarpino!" Lenore squealed. "I can't believe it! He actually talked to me! I wish my parents let me have social media so I could post this!"

"This whole weekend feels surreal," Cass said. "Also, you can print those selfies for your locker and binders."

"You're a genius, Cass Felicity Fairchild!" Lenore walked to her door, ready to print her new photos at the family computer.

"Hey Lenore, I know you're on cloud nine, but can we talk about the problem we have?"

"What problem?"

"For one thing, we never finished searching the house. As soon as Kevin came in, all attention was on him," Cass said, noticing her friend's smile grow when she said the musician's name. "We are missing clues! How can we identify this mystery woman and her motives, relations, or alibi when it comes to Mr. Benson? How many secrets was he keeping? Secondly, I still have the cigarette packs and vodka bottles in my purse!" Cass was panicking. "You have a gross kissing letter on you! What if we get grounded or arrested?!"

"It's okay, Cass," Lenore said. "We got a lot from today–those letters have so much. If we really really need more clues, we can always ask a prospective homebuyer if we can search again. Also, I have an idea for those adult items. Let's just help take out the trash."

Mrs. Hurley was shocked at Lenore's eagerness to do chores, but still let her grab the trash bags from all the rooms in the house. Lenore tore the letter detailing Ruby and Coffee Bean's kisses into pieces and threw it into her room's trash bag. She then threw the cigarettes and mini vodka bottles in Jennie and Jeanine's nighttime underwear trash bag, so her parents would be too disgusted if they were suspicious of her motives. She then put it all in the garbage can and wheeled it out to the street for the next day's trash collection.

"See?" Lenore said as she pushed the trash can to the curb. "All done."

"Okay, but should we get back to investigating?"

"Yeah, after I print those photos of Kevin Scarpino with us. Can you email them to me?"

✳✳✳

Of course another shooting would happen the day of the open house. Detective Gomez had wanted to get there early, before people dropped in and he couldn't get on his knees to check for any loose boards. He finished filling out his paperwork for the day and drove out to Mr. Benson's house with an hour left for the event.

The realtor enthusiastically approached him as he walked to the front door.

"Hello, welcome to our open house today," she said, reaching out her hand. "My name is Jan Schuur. Let me know if you have any questions. A few people are interested in making an offer."

Gomez showed her his detective badge.

"Thank you," he started his spiel. "My name is Detective David Gomez, and I am investigating the murder of Edward Benson. I heard old houses like his have removable floorboards and was wondering if I could investigate discreetly."

Jan's smile faded as she dutifully led him upstairs and looked out for potential homebuyers on that floor. He felt for loose boards with his feet when one squeaked gently. He kneeled down and pulled at the board.

It was empty, but when he used his flashlight he noticed some dust particles giving away hand prints. Someone had been here before him. He took a sample of the fingerprints and continued walking on the hardwood floors upstairs.

Detective Gomez told Jan once he was ready to move to the downstairs area. The house was almost empty, so Jan grabbed the last couple lingering and moved them to the porch to answer their questions. Gomez set about feeling for the loose boards in the hallway, the bathroom, and the kitchen. Nothing again.

He took a deep breath again and tried the dining room. It took him five steps, but he found the squeak. He knelt down and loosened the board.

He took his flashlight out and it shined on some letters and an old picture of a young-looking woman smiling in a bikini at the beach. The back of the photo said, "Me, 1965." He grabbed the letter to read it. The yellowed paper's tiny, blue cursive handwriting was hard to make out.

"Dearest Coffee Bean,

Please be patient. This is taking longer than I thought. The dud keeps insisting we travel everywhere now that I'm better. Maybe I'll send you a postcard from Las Vegas, if he delivers.

We're so close to being together, I can taste it. At some point he'll get bored of me again, and I'll be all yours. We'll get together and get out of here, happily ever after. We'll finally be able to—"

Det. Gomez felt himself speeding through the letter after reading about passionate kissing, until he got to something less intimate.

"Give the boys kisses for me. I can't wait to see you all soon.

Love,

Your Ruby"

Chapter Twenty-Five

Lenore skipped into Moon Town Middle School. She put both photos of her with Kevin Scarpino and the one with Cass in her locker first thing before shoving her backpack in and going to the gym. It took one "hey" from Katie to get her rambling

"I met Kevin Scarpino yesterday!" Lenore squealed.

"*We* met Kevin Scarpino yesterday," Cass snickered as she got in the locker room. "We found clues for our murder mystery."

"You're both just making that up since you don't want to talk about slow dancing with eighth graders!" Katie said.

"No way!" Lenore said. "He seriously was looking at Mr. Benson's house!"

Cass grabbed her smartphone she was hiding in her locker and pulled up the photos for the class to ogle at.

"He's so dreamy," Katie said looking at the pics. "Fine, you're telling the truth, but that still doesn't mean we aren't going to ask you about dancing with Noah Thompson!"

"I thought he was single, okay!" Lenore defended.

"And did you dance with Leo Fernandez, Cass?" Katie asked.

BaDUM. Cass' heart took a leap. Crap. *Think of something else to say.*

"We met Kevin Scarpino this weekend, Katie," Cass said, deflecting.

Despite their friends being interested in them meeting Kevin Scarpino, everyone stopped caring by lunch. Cass and Lenore were secluding themselves from everyone at the lunch table and talking about the case.

"So, I think we should narrow down possible secret lovers," Cass said. "I think it's obvious to say he asked for that money from Marnie Woodson to help pay for the mystery woman's illness."

"I wonder what kind of illness it was," Lenore said.

"It probably was something like MS or Parkinson's?"

"I don't think either of those are curable."

"Fair. Maybe like a long cold or a broken bone. It's really hard for old people to heal from those."

"Maybe. Could we think of any old ladies who were sick in the last few years?"

"Maybe, but we need to see how far back that affair was. We should ask Ms. Woodson how long back Mr. Benson asked for money. We know where she lives, and I can probably pop by her house this week."

"I probably can't join you this week. My mom set up a bunch of doctor's appointments after school for me, from the dentist to the eye doctor."

Just then, the lunch bell rang. The girls walked to math class. Cass physically felt okay but was starting to be concerned. She felt simultaneously like she was in her body, but not. It was hard to concentrate in class. Maybe the case was causing this? Somehow, the rest of the day flew by, and Cass waited with Lenore to get picked up by their respective parents.

"Could your neighbors have been potential lovers with him?" Cass asked as she stood with Lenore outside the school.

"Gross," Lenore replied. "Who would do it with him?"

"Someone calling him a coffee bean, apparently. Maybe the woman's husband killed him."

"Ooh, that's a good guess. Just where would we get the proof?"

"Still not sure."

Mrs. Hurley honked her minivan's horn a few times before Lenore saw her mom and got into the car. Cass sighed.

Cass was stuck in after-school study hall for the next few hours, waiting for either of her parents to arrive. She finished her homework since the workload was light, and grew bored. Lenore had the mystery notebook with her so Cass didn't know what to do with her time. She grabbed some notebook paper and began writing down all the elderly married women Mr. Benson could have been dating. First was maybe Marnie from the church, then both Mrs. Stark and Mrs. Jepsen, since they lived nearby. Then who else?

She'd try to call Ted Jr. and Allison later.

She kept staring at the paper as if something was going to jump out to her when a surprise voice made her leap in her seat.

"Hey, Cass, what's up?" Leo Fernandez said from behind her. "Did I scare you?"

"A little," Cass blushed. "What are you doing here?"

"Just waiting for my dad to get me. He's running late from work."

"What does your dad do?"

"He teaches high school anatomy," he said. "Apparently today was a test day so he's grading. Sorry if I'm distracting you."

"No, I actually finished homework a half hour ago. I'm just studying."

"Studying what? The murder?"

Cass' heart began racing. His brown eyes looked down at her sheet of paper. She noticed his plain green t-shirt complimented his eyes. She wanted to keep staring at him but she also wanted to impress him.

"Yes," she said, after realizing it had been a few seconds since he asked.

"Cool! How's it going?"

Cass paused.

"Kinda slow… Do you want to help?"

"Sure. What's the facts?"

Cass caught Leo up to the present, skipping the parts about her premonitions and feelings. She avoided talking about the vodka, cigarettes, the kissing letter, and—honestly—all the parts that involved her and Lenore lying their butts off to authority and being told not to investigate. Leo nodded encouragingly.

"Oh, a paramour?" Leo asked.

"Paramore? Like 'Misery Business'?"

"Not the band," Leo corrected. "The French word for secret lover."

"Yeah, I should have known that."

"So, have you and Lenore gone over the new evidence?" he asked.

"Well, I was just brainstorming this afternoon since she had a dentist appointment," Cass said. "I'll probably talk to her later, but she seems to be too distracted this weekend to help me pin down a secret lover for Mr. Benson."

"Well, it isn't everyday a star looks to move back to his hometown," Leo joked. "Do you think if she got a restraining order her family would have to move houses?"

Cass laughed, not surprised her friend's bragging had spread around the school like glitter on a craft project.

"She'll calm down," Cass said. "I think."

"Maybe the paramour is from his old hometown," Leo suggested. "Like he moved to cover his tracks, and the other guy found out a few months ago and then stabbed him."

"That's a pretty good theory," Cass smiled in excitement. "We have both of his kids' numbers. His son hates him, but his daughter seemed nice when we interacted with her at the funeral."

Right then, she got a call from her mom saying she was outside the entrance. Cass hung up and grabbed her papers. Leo got up with her and grabbed his things as he put his phone in his pocket.

"My mom's here," Cass said.

"So's my dad. Walk together?"

They both signed out of study hall and walked to the front.

"Well, if you need any help with finding this mystery woman, I'd be happy to help."

"Yeah, that'd be great."

They both stared at each other, not sure whether to hug or handshake or wave as Mrs. Fairchild stood ten feet away with Lucy strapped to her chest. Leo broke the ice with a wave and walked away.

"Oh, is that a new friend?" Mrs. Fairchild asked as they walked to the parking lot.

"Yeah," Cass muttered.

"Wait. You're a little red in the ears. Is that the same Leo from the dance?"

"Mom, can we wait till the car for questions?"

Chapter Twenty-Six

Cass took a deep breath. She looked at her phone, which had the numbers all typed out to call Mrs. Allison Carter nee Benson.

All she remembered saying to her at the funeral was "sorry for your loss"; "thanks for the cat"; and "sorry, just want to get to the brownies."

The only reason she had the woman's number was because Ted Jr. had given it to her when they went to clean out Mr. Benson's house.

She stared at the phone for a few minutes more until the screen went black. What if she didn't answer? What if she hung up on her like Ted Jr. did? What if she cursed her out?

Suddenly, something soft and fuzzy rubbed against her elbow. Elroy was there, demanding pats on the head and scratches behind the ears. Cass petted him until a sense of normalcy returned to her.

Cass told herself to bite the bullet of cold calling and clicked the call button on her screen. She took a deep breath in. The phone rang. Cass breathed out. The phone rang again. Cass breathed in again. The number started to dial, but then she heard—

"Hello, this is Allison. Who's speaking?"

Cass held her breath, forgetting what she was doing.

"Hello?" Allison asked again. Cass breathed out quickly.

"Hi, this is Cass Fairchild. We met at your dad's funeral. Can you talk right now?"

"Sure, Cass. What's going on?"

"Well, my best friend and I are investigating your father's murder, and we came across another stumbling block and could use your help. Was there any chance your dad was dating someone else while he was in Danville, Kentucky?"

An awkward pause ensued.

"Not that your dad was a dirty cheater or anything," Cass further rambled. "It's because we found these love letters he had received without dates on the top of them. I guess he called the mystery woman his 'Ruby' and she called him 'Coffee Bean.' Also, some people here said he wanted to take dance classes and had a twinkle in his eyes when talking about it. Unless I'm totally wrong, and your dad just really liked dancing and was trying to get back into dancing because exercise is always good."

Cass breathed out as she heard Allison pause on the other end.

"My parents were attached at the hip till the day my mom died," Allison said softly. "It would have been impossible for him to have an affair unless he wanted Mom to know."

"Well, hypothetically speaking, when your mom died did anyone reach out to him? Like family friends? My mom's brother's friend married a woman after her husband died. Not right after. She was just lonely and he wanted to comfort her and then things happened. Not bad things. It was all respectful. Steve and Margaret are great. Not that you know them. Oh gosh, I'm rambling, I'm so sorry. I'm getting off track."

Allison left out a soft, genuine laugh.

"You're okay, honey. You actually sound like one of my kids right now," she said. "He's eighteen, and he rambles when he thinks he's in trouble. You're fine, I get what you mean. My parents had a lot of couples friends, but they outlived most of them.

"My father had the same secretary for twenty years, but she quit as soon as she hit retirement and didn't keep in touch when she and her husband moved to Colorado.

"My father was a good person, but growing up I could always tell he was a little bored with the area. My mom loved Kentucky and never wanted to move, so he listened to her. When she died of cancer ten years ago, he was crushed. My parents perfectly complemented each other. She liked sweet food, he liked spicy. He liked the cold, she preferred the heat. As much as he loved her, I understood why he moved away like he did when she died. The memories were too much, and he didn't want to live in this state, anyway." She took a deep breath.

"At first, some of his old friends would try to approach Ted and I, saying they missed him, but those men's wives never seemed too upset. My brother always gets upset at the subject of Dad moving, but I think he was too hurt from our childhood to understand him as an adult. But anyways, our dad probably wasn't seeing anyone from here when he died. I'm a little surprised you said he has letters. Dad's handwriting was messy and illegible most of the time. I once got a postcard from him after he moved. It's a picture of the Carnegie Museum of Art on one side, and I still can't read what he wrote on the back.

"Whoever this mystery woman is, she must have reignited something in him, I can tell you that. My husband and I would try to make him come out for the holidays, and he usually refused. The last few years his excuse for avoiding us was that he had some plans. I hope this helps."

Cass looked at Elroy snuggling against her, purring like a lawnmower.

"Yeah, it helps close a theory," Cass said. "My friend once told me when you eliminate the possible, whatever's left is the answer."

"Ah, Sherlock Holmes," Allison said. "He's a good consultant."

"Well, I got that line from my friend Lenore, but she probably got it from him, so yeah."

Chapter Twenty-Seven

"Since she doesn't hate her dad, we can scratch out my own theory that Allison killed Mr. Benson after realizing he was having an affair," Lenore said the next morning after Cass brought up last night's phone call.

The girls walked into the gym and began stretching before the final bell rang.

"Why would she hate him for that? If their mother was long gone, there's no motivation."

"True, but we also don't have any motive for the murder."

Cass was cut off by the Pledge of Allegiance and morning announcements. The conversation was further broken up by Coach Webber putting the girls on opposite teams for kickball. Lenore and Cass were about to talk at first base, but the former ran off after her teammate kicked a home run.

Finally at lunch, they pulled out the mystery notebook with their lunch boxes.

"Murders have means, motives, and opportunities," Lenore said, writing out the key words. "We know he was stabbed to death, so," she wrote "stabbed by kitchen knife" under "Means."

"The motive," she said as she drew an X over the word. "We

don't know."

"The opportunity." Cass spoke up. "Everyone we talked to had an alibi."

Lenore crossed out the word.

"Maybe someone was lying," Lenore said, looking up from the notebook. "Maybe we interviewed the killer, but they are a good liar and we didn't notice."

"But Lenore," Cass started. "If we don't trust these people, doesn't that mean all our information is wrong and we're back to square one?"

"It's okay, we took notes on your precog right? So, we still have that information," Lenore said.

Cass grabbed the notebook.

"Let's not do anything hastily," she warned.

She felt really protective over the notebook suddenly and was worried Lenore might tear out the pages.

"I feel like my precog gets it wrong. Like that time I stared at that lady in church and thought she was at the funeral and she wasn't."

"Yeah, but us approaching Betty Green pointed us to both Trevor Gibbons and Marnie Woodson. Both gave valuable information. By the way, are you available this afternoon to ask Marnie if she knew when she gave money to Mr. Benson?"

"Yeah, I can do that," Cass forced the notebook in her backpack.

"Why are you being overly caring about the mystery notebook?"

"I just feel the need to protect it."

"So, you're feeling you need to save it? Is your precog acting up?"

"Maybe."

"Okay, now I'm glad I didn't grab my scissors out of my pencil case to cut out pages. So the case is going the way it's supposed to."

"I suppose."

"Maybe we can talk to Betty this week and try to interview

her again, too. Maybe we moved on too fast from that intuition," Lenore offered.

"That's true," Cass said. "I don't know if I can come over this week, can you handle it on your own?"

Lenore laughed. "Yeah, I'm The Great Lenore Hurley! You're The Awesome Cass Fairchild who can talk to Marnie, too."

Cass appreciated Lenore's confidence but wasn't so sure about being awesome.

✳✳✳

Cass told her mom she was going out for a walk that afternoon after school. The neighborhood her family lived in had big houses with plenty of sidewalks, but it still creeped Cass out since they all almost looked the same. The only differences were due to the homeowners' creativity when it came to decorated porches and gardens.

After seeing the fifth blue colonial house, Cass tried to retrace her steps. She remembered taking a certain path to Marnie Woodson's house and thought she'd taken a left after a blue house with *two* garden gnomes. This house had a bird bath and feeder, but no gnomes.

Cass started feeling unsure of her abilities. She stood there on the pavement for a few minutes, nervous that she was attracting attention from the neighbors staring out their windows as she stared at the ground. But she really wanted to do this without help from strangers or her precog.

She gave up as a squirrel jumped onto the house's bird feeder. Cass pulled out her cell phone and searched for Marnie's address. After two minutes, she got the right address and followed her GPS to Marnie's house.

She put her phone down once she was at the right house. Cass noticed the blue SUV parked in the driveway and the fall harvest "Welcome" sign on the door. This was right. But as she approached the front door, her heart started pounding. She wanted to walk forward, but something innate whispered at her to turn back.

Only trouble lies ahead. You're in danger. This is dangerous. Go away. Go away. Go away.

Cass felt light years away from the doorbell even though she was standing ten feet from it.

Cass struggled to take breaths as her heart kept pounding. *BaDUM. BaDUM. BaDUM. BaDUM.* Why couldn't she breathe?

She got five feet from the doorbell, but now the thoughts were screaming *"DON'T DO IT, GO AWAY, DON'T YOU DARE DO IT!"*

Cass looked at the doorbell and pressed it, but her legs stopped listening to her and she ran away in tears. What the heck was wrong with her?

She sat behind the blue house with the gnomes and let the tears rush out of her eyes. Nothing good was coming of this murder investigation.

What on earth was she doing? No adult would believe her or Lenore if they ever solved the mystery. They were only kids. All they know is that some person killed Mr. Benson, and the murderer was too smart to be tracked. No amount of good people would help them. Cass was now shaking and sob-breathing. Knowing when Mr. Benson asked for a handout wasn't going to break open the case. Cass felt ashamed for peeking into Mr. Benson's business. Her parents told her all the time to keep her nose out of others' lives. Everyone had told her to mind her business or else, and what did all this do? Nothing.

There was no moving forward. Cass continued crying for a few minutes when a couple who looked to be in their thirties were suddenly in front of her.

"Hey, are you okay?" the man asked, concerned.

"Are you lost?" the woman followed up.

Cass wiped the tears from her eyes and snot from her nose.

She nodded and gave a small "I'm fine" before breaking out into a sprint back home. Of course, it was when she was running that she realized the path back home. Cass quietly closed the door and hurried back upstairs to her room to fix her appearance before any of her family members approached her. Nothing was okay.

CHAPTER TWENTY-EIGHT

One ring and the phone picked up.

"Hello?"

"Hi, Mrs. Jepsen. Do you have the Greens number?" Lenore asked.

"Hi, Lenore," Mrs. Jepsen said. "Let me get my address book."

Lenore heard silence for a few minutes.

"Okay, I have it now," Mrs. Jepsen said. "How is the case going?"

"It's alright. I hope Mrs. Green has some more info to give me."

"Just you?"

"Yeah, Cass is doing other stuff."

"Is she over this case?"

"No! Why would she be?" Lenore asked, a little surprised.

"Oh, sorry for touching a nerve there," Mrs. Jepsen said. "She just seemed distracted on Sunday, like she was tired of chasing feelings."

"She didn't say that to me!" Lenore got a little defensive. "You were talking to that nice blonde man, Kevin Sardino."

"Kevin Scarpino," Lenore corrected. "I mean, she is doing her own case work right now. She wants justice for Mr. Benson, too."

"Of course she does," Mrs. Jepsen said in a soothing voice. "Would you like Betty's number again?"

"Oh, yeah!" Lenore said.

Lenore looked at the back of her math notebook where she'd written her questions. She could've really used the mystery notebook right now. She punched the numbers into her family's cordless landline. The phone rang four times before she heard, "This is the Greens. We're not here right now, but if you leave your name and number, we'll get back with you as soon as we can. Have a blessed day."

Sigh, Lenore breathed out.

✷✷✷

The detective put his stained Moon Town PD coffee cup down on his boss' desk. This was an interesting conversation.

"So, there was some truth to those churchgoers' gossip," Sgt. Henry Fuller told Gomez that Monday. "Old man had a lover."

Gomez was still waiting to hear back from CSI about the letter and dust collection. The investigators said they were having a hard time unmixing what looked like two fingerprints overlapped.

He sat at his sergeant's desk almost expecting to be given another case for the week.

"Well ADA Hurley's daughter is also investigating, so we seem behind," Gomez said.

"Do you think this kid may be withholding evidence from us?"

"With her best friend, yes."

"Do you think what they know can solve this case?"

"You're gonna make me intimidate some middle schoolers. Is

that correct sir?"

"That I am, but also don't make them cry. We don't want Hurley coming over from Pittsburgh to yell at us."

✳✳✳

Cass and Lenore were almost crying tears of boredom in Mrs. Leary's class that day. Their teacher kept droning on and on about participles and verb forms. Cass couldn't stop thinking about what happened to her the previous day with her breakdown.

Why was she so scared at Marnie's house? There was no way she would have felt that way if Marnie was innocent. The woman was too nice.

But also, what if her feelings were not related to the case? Maybe her feelings weren't related to any of what was going on?

Cass didn't like that thought. It would have made everything a waste.

Cass wasn't ready to tell Lenore about what happened because every time she thought about it, she was ready to cry again. The margins of her notebook were filled with little tornadoes rushing to wipe out her grammar notes.

Before she could further berate herself, she and the rest of the class were distracted by Mrs. Leary's class landline ringing. The old lady huffed as she walked to the phone on the wall.

"Hello?" she said. "Okay, I will."

Mrs. Leary hung up and turned back to the class.

"Miss Fairchild, Miss Hurley, the front office needs you. Grab some hall passes and don't lollygag."

Everyone made "oohs" as the girls got up from their desks.

"We're not in trouble, are we?" Cass asked her best friend as they walked to the office.

"Nah," Lenore replied. "Probably just Miss Barber checking on us again or something."

Lenore opened the office door and they were directed to the guidance counselor's office.

"Just like I predicted," Lenore said.

She opened the door and Cass' stomach flipped at the sight of Detective Gomez and Miss Barber staring at them. The latter somehow looked scarier than the actual police officer, shooting daggers from her eyes and straightening her posture. The detective stood casually behind the desk with a vacant look in his eyes.

"Girls, sit down," Miss Barber said.

Both took the available seats in front of the guidance counselor's desk.

"You're not in trouble, but do you both know why you're here?" Barber asked.

"Because Detective Gomez cares about murder victim's families so much, he likes to check up on those who also attended the funeral," Lenore offered.

"No!" Miss Barber angrily let out. "It's because you two are still investigating an open homicide case even after I specifically told you not to do it!"

Lenore's mouth dropped in fake outrage. She figured they'd eventually be caught by an authority, but not this quickly.

"In our defense, we didn't think we'd be caught," Lenore said. "Also, nowhere in the Constitution does it say we can't investigate a murder that happened near my backyard."

Miss Barber looked like she was going to suspend Lenore for talking back.

"Girls," the detective cut in. "It's fine," he directed at the guidance counselor before turning to the girls. "But, if you have any evidence or useful information you're withholding from the police, you need to give it to me now. This is official police business. I'm going off my detective senses right now that you were both at the open house Sunday. And I'm also deducing you both found a hidden floor board full of evidence you took home with you."

"No polygraphs, no statements, no waivers," Lenore said confidently. "Also, I would like to speak with my lawyer, AKA my dad. Miss Barber, can I use your phone?"

Both adults looked at each other, unsure what to do with a child correctly citing the law.

"You know what Miss Hurley, you can take that attitude with you back to class," Miss Barber said.

"So, we're free to go then?"

The adults looked at each other again, not sure what to do. Gomez had a suspicion from knowing Lenore's father—and talking to her mother for a little while—that she would be difficult to get information from. Maybe he would ask her nervous-looking best friend, shaking in her chair.

"Yes, you can," the counselor suddenly announced. "But this is an open case, and any interference with police work will get you in trouble."

Miss Barber gave him a glare, hoping for approval. She reached out and touched his right arm lightly.

"Right, David?"

He was a little taken aback as he heard the light snorts from the girls. He knew she was trying to help, but her interpersonal communication skills were pretty weak.

The girls got up from their seats and started walking back to class.

"Where'd you get that line about the lawyers?" Cass asked her best friend.

"My mom gave it to me a few years ago," Lenore said. "She was pulled over when my sisters were still newborn babies. She didn't get a ticket, but she was so mad at the whole interaction she turned around, looked me dead in the eyes, and said if the police ever detained me to say what I just did."

"Wow," Cass said, looking toward the bathroom as they got closer to Mrs. Leary's classroom. "Hey, I have to go to the bathroom."

"Okay, I'll make something up to Mrs. Weary."

Cass walked into the bathroom and stared at herself in the mirror. She was too scared to talk to the police, but too scared to go back to class. She didn't feel right inside. She wasn't ready to just let go of this case without getting any closure.

She took a deep breath, washed her face, and left the bathroom. Cass looked around and saw Detective Gomez swiftly walk toward her. Nothing she could do now.

"Miss Fairchild, please wait," he pleaded. "If you have anything you can give us, we'd really be pleased. And you won't get in trouble no matter what you tell us."

Cass stared at him, unsure how to respond. She looked at him, but felt herself distracted by the drop ceiling lights of the school. Why did she suddenly feel out of her body again?

"It's okay, miss, you and your friend are not in trouble."

"I know, I just get nervous when I talk to the police," Cass said. "I know you're not going to arrest me, but the sight of officers always makes me feel like I'm in trouble. I don't know why, but the school made me sit with our SRO for a few lunches last year because they were worried I was afraid of the police. And I'm not, it's just… What if I'm doing something bad? I don't want an arrest on my record. What am I even doing?"

"It's okay, but if you ever want to talk…" he pulled out a business card. "Call me. Any information helps."

He walked away and Cass went back into the bathroom to compose herself before returning to Mrs. Leary's class. She took her regular seat and noticed Lenore winking at her. After the bell rang, the girls walked to their lockers.

"So, what's up?" Lenore asked. "I told Mrs. Leary your monthly gift just arrived. But don't worry, I pulled her aside and whispered it so you wouldn't be embarrassed."

"Wow, thanks," Cass said. "I don't know. I left the bathroom when that detective approached me. He gave me his business card and told me to call him."

"Gross."

"Yeah, I don't really want to tell him about all the trouble we've been through."

"Exactly! We don't want to give all that we've been investigating away to some guy who will get all the recognition and glory when *we* solve it. All we'd get is my parents nagging for nothing."

"Yeah, but what if he knows something we don't?"

"So? He has CSI at his job. He can't have unearthed much. It's best to throw that card away and get on with the case without him. By the way, did you see him react to Miss Barber grabbing his arm?"

"So awkward," Cass laughed.

"Could she be any more obvious?" Lenore laughed before switching the subject. "By the way, I tried to call Mrs. Green this week but got voicemail. Did you talk to Marnie this week?"

"No I didn't get around to it," Cass shrugged.

"Why not?"

"I just didn't," Cass snapped.

"Okay, okay, take it easy," Lenore said. "It's fine. I can call her later if you're busy."

"You probably should."

✳✳✳

Cass couldn't sleep as usual that night, unsure how to go on with the case. Detective Gomez was stoic-faced, but he probably knew more than them and urgently needed to connect the dots.

Cass sat up in bed. She wasn't sure what to do. Then Elroy wandered in her room, mewing softly. He walked up to her, sniffed her left hand, and demanded head pats. She petted him for a bit, then decided it was time to actually try to sleep. But the cat was being so sweet. She didn't want him to run away. Cass petted him without realizing thirty minutes had passed in the dark. Elroy finished the petting session by settling himself next to her legs.

Cass admired his cute, sleepy self and figured she should follow his lead.

Cass was suddenly asleep. She was standing with the trees hundreds of feet above her as the maple leaves fell down. Cass was bundled up as if it was about to snow, even though it seemed early. Cass observed the red leaves turn brown suddenly as they hit the ground. Suddenly Mr. Benson's body was lying in front of her, half a foot of foliage gathered above his body, his pale stiff face exposed. His lips were moving slowly.

Cass tried bending over and still couldn't hear him. She got on her knees to listen.

"Keep going," he whispered.

The leaves changed into snow flakes around them. Snow collected over Benson's face.

Cass had to put her right ear to his mouth to hear him softly mutter.

"Keep going, Cass."

She woke up fifteen minutes before her alarm. She scrolled on her smartphone for a minute. She then went over to her folded jeans from the day before and pulled them up. She fished through her front pockets until she found what she needed and pulled the card out. Cass typed in the number gingerly, stared at the message keyboard, and decided to text.

"Hi, sir. This is Cass Fairchild. Can we talk privately about the case soon?"

Chapter Twenty-Nine

The phone kept ringing.

Ring. Ring. Ring.

"Hello?" Mrs. Green picked up. "Who is speaking?"

"Hi, Mrs. Green, it's me, Lenore Hurley. We met after church that one time."

Lenore was sitting at her desk in her room. The little talk with Detective Gomez and Miss Barber had motivated her to keep calling everyone. Marnie was easy to call that afternoon. But Mrs. Green was her white whale.

"How are you dear?"

"I'm good. I just need a little help with the case."

"Case?"

"Yeah, Mr. Benson's murder case!"

"Oh!" Mrs. Green shuddered. "How dreadful!"

"I know," Lenore said. "I want to ask what you and Mr. Green were doing the night of the murder?"

"We were out to dinner in Pittsburgh."

"You really wanted to drive all the way to the city for dinner?"

"Yes," Mrs. Green affirmed. "We celebrate my surviving a

stroke at Tony's Italian there every year."

Lenore was so surprised, she wasn't sure how to respond.

"Uh, congrats," Lenore said.

"Thank you," Mrs. Green said. "I couldn't walk right for months. It took some intense treatment and experimental stuff. Now, I don't want to be considered a suspect in your little murder game."

Lenore tried to apologize as Mrs. Green slammed the phone down. Well, this was definitely going into the mystery notebook.

✳✳✳

Cass slowed her pace as she walked through Moon Town Middle the next morning, her thoughts weighing her down like a ball and chain strapped at her ankle. Lenore skipped up to her at the locker room to share her findings from calling Marnie the night before, before talking to Betty.

"The woman said she remembers giving the money to Mr. Benson about two years ago," Lenore said a little loudly. "Maybe that's how old the letters are!"

"Yeah," Cass said tiredly.

"I think the next thing to do is probably look back at the churchgoers and my neighbors. Or maybe search obituaries?"

"Yeah," Cass said, dazed.

"You okay?"

"I'm fine," Cass lied.

"Okay, so get this. I also got a hold of Betty Green last night, and she hung up on me!" Lenore said with a little outrage.

"What?" Cass looked up at Lenore.

"Yeah!" Lenore said. "But she also said she survived a stroke years ago and has been recovering since. And 'Ruby' is also recovering from something two years ago. Maybe there's a correlation."

"That's really good, Lenore!"

"I know right! Add it to the mystery notebook."

"I think I left that in my locker," Cass lied. The notebook was in her backpack, resting against her history binder. Cass looked away from her friend and hoped she didn't notice. She felt like the biggest traitor.

Time dragged for Cass before she finally got to lunch. After scarfing down a sandwich and chips, Cass told Lenore she had to go to the bathroom, then walked to her locker, and pulled out her backpack. She felt bad walking away from her friend and reneging on their agreement from yesterday, but she wanted to solve this case for Mr. Benson. And the only way to solve this case was to try something different.

For Mr. Benson. For Mr. Benson. For Mr. Benson. Her thoughts kept ringing in her head. *For Mr. Benson. For Mr. Benson. For Mr. Benson. OW!*

Cass realized she walked into the front office door. She took two steps back and entered the office—this time gracefully.

"Are you okay, hon?" the secretary asked, trying to get up from her desk.

"Yeah, I just got lost in thought," Cass fake laughed. "I have a meeting in Miss Barber's office."

"Go right ahead."

Cass was too nervous to open the door, but also too afraid not to open it. Everything was about to change. She stared at it for a minute before completely swinging it open.

Detective Gomez was sitting in Miss Barber's chair, leaning it back as he stretched. He hit a tall plant she kept by the window. He snapped back and stood up at the sight of Cass entering.

"Um, hi, sir," she said, quickly. She took a little sigh of relief that Miss Barber wasn't there, entertaining as it was to watch her interact with the detective.

"Miss Fairchild, please take a seat," he still stood, gesturing to the usual chair she'd sat in many times before.

"You can just call me Cass. So, how can I help you? Or I guess you help me, or whatever," she blabbered.

"Help the police, Miss Cass," he said politely. "So, tell me everything you know about the case, starting from when we first met at the scene of the crime."

Cass hesitated for a second, wondering what Lenore would say if she found out her friend narc'd to the cops. It was probably better to get everything out in the open so the crime would be solved, rather than keeping what she knew inside and struggling to find answers. She told Detective Gomez everything from Lenore's neighbors to the churchgoers. She told him about the possible lover, the debt, and the hidden floor board—including the cigarettes and alcohol and the awkward letter. She made sure to emphasize that they had thrown out all of that stuff, and she hadn't been vulnerable to peer pressure.

The detective nodded along to her story from time to time, never interrupting while making small notes. He listened to her as she went on about her feelings guiding their expeditions and the mystery notebook. Once Cass finished talking she took a deep breath.

"So, yeah," she concluded. "I think that's all."

"Do you have any of those other letters from Mr. Benson's lover on you?" the detective asked.

"Yeah, are you going to take them?" Cass asked.

"Well, yes, I need them to solve the case. Do you want copies of them?"

"Lenore isn't going to like this," Cass said as she pulled the mystery notebook out of her backpack. She flipped to the pages where they had stapled the letters.

"Miss Hurley's feelings do not affect the case, Miss Cass. It looks like your guidance counselor has a photocopier here if you want to keep the doubles," he said, grabbing the papers and walking over to the machine. "Speaking of which, why did you text me this morning ready to talk?"

Cass told him about the dream she had, and he nodded in understanding.

"I hate dreaming while working on these types of cases," he said. "I try not to dream."

He handed her back the photo copies of the letters.

"Can I ask you something?" Cass said as Detective Gomez sat back down.

"Sure."

"Why do you need our information? Are you also struggling with the case?"

Gomez smiled a little.

"Can't say, but when it comes to cold cases, we really rely on the help of neighbors and anyone with information."

"Okay, so you're probably still lost. Any idea on a suspect?"

"I have suspects."

"Who?"

"Police business. Now, I need to ask you something. You say you investigate and lead off your feelings? What does that mean?"

"We go off my feelings when it comes to cases. Like the time we went to Mr. Benson's church service, I saw this woman and couldn't stop thinking it could be her. My heart kept racing. I kept hearing she had to be the woman from the funeral. But then it turned out she wasn't the person who attended, but she knew people who went and also knew Mr. Benson. Also, the day we found his body, I remember having this sense of doom go through me. Like something was happening, so we decided to investigate."

"What were you doing when you felt this sense of doom?" Detective Gomez interrupted.

Cass paused for a second to remember that day.

"Uh, math homework."

"Ah," he said. "Continue."

"So we checked with Lenore's family first, and then went outside and moved in the direction based on how bad I felt. We actually overshot Mr. Benson's body by a lot, but if I hadn't felt that bad and we hadn't turned around, then we wouldn't have spotted his body sticking out from the area."

"Wow," Detective Gomez said. "So, you go off your clues by using anxiety."

"Anxiety? What's that?" Cass asked. "It's based more on a feeling," she paused before admitting her secret. At this point she told him everything else. "Like I'm psychic."

"You're not psychic. Your mind is telling you that you're not okay in otherwise calm situations," Detective Gomez calmly replied. "Have you ever told your parents about this?"

"And get poked and prodded by doctors? No, thank you."

"Hear me out, Miss Cass. Do you get these feelings when doing something you're uncomfortable with or are nervous about? Like, the thought of tests or deadlines? Do you ever get a racing heart when you're not doing anything? And I mean nothing at all? Not exercising in any way, but rather at your desk reading a book."

This was turning into a full blown personal confession, and Cass was done answering his questions. How did he exactly know what was going on with her? How dare he act like he knew what she was going through.

Detective Gomez opened his mouth again.

"I know about this because my younger sister has anxiety, and from the way she acted when she was about your age, it's not much different from what you're describing. She would always think her appendix was bursting," he said. "You think the world is ending but all these feelings—they're all in your head. They're not real."

"I don't have anxiety, you can't prove that," Cass said, suddenly standing up. She fought the urge to grab her throbbing right arm in front of him.

"You're right. I can't," he said. "But I know if you want those thoughts that keep you up at night to go away, you should probably talk to your parents."

"Okay, well, goodbye Detective Gomez," she said as she hurried out the door.

Cass checked the time on the hall's clock before going to her locker to get her books for Mrs. Leary's class. She quietly closed the classroom door and went to her seat without interruption. Like clockwork, Lenore turned around and made a face at her. Cass smiled back as she pulled out her English binder.

After the final bell, Cass walked back to her locker quickly with Lenore in tow. She really didn't want to lie to her best friend again.

"Hey, where did you go? Why'd you miss math class?" her friend pestered.

"I had a meeting at Miss Barber's office," Cass said. "It went kinda long."

"What does that crazy woman want from us? Has she not learned we're gonna solve this case before she even realizes it?"

"Yeah, I don't know," Cass said as she turned her locker's combination.

"So, I was thinking in Mrs. Leary's class about how Mrs. Green was so mad," Lenore said. "I really think she could be our killer."

"Why?"

"Think about it: She could have been just covering up about not knowing him in front of us and the Starks, and she is also recovering from something like Ruby was. And she was allegedly 'out for dinner in Pittsburgh' the night of the murder."

"You didn't get to talk to her much, though, last night."

"But think of church! She also wore *burgundy,* and you know the mysterious lover calls herself 'Your Ruby.' She probably has a red theme in her closet."

"That's a good point," Cass said. They started walking to the car line outside.
"I know! Thanks. I think you actually picked her out as the murderer with those strong vibes at church. If that isn't an indicator, I don't know what that is."

Cass looked for her mom in the car line, hoping to get out of the conversation.

"I don't know," Cass shrugged. She thought she saw her

mom's car near the end of the block.

"It is!" Lenore cheered. "Your psychic prowess is solving the case."

"I think I see my mom," Cass went. "I got to go."

"Bye!"

"And I don't know about that psychic prowess," Cass muttered as she walked away.

Chapter Thirty

Cass spiralled as she stared at her phone that afternoon. She Googled "anxiety" after locking her bedroom door.

Detective Gomez' words stuck with her.

The first thing to pop up said anxiety was a normal emotion to have. She smiled until she saw the next line say that the disproportionate amount of that emotion was a disorder.

Cass scrolled through the search results' checklist of anxiety symptoms for twelve-year-old girls. Insomnia? Check. Random feelings of pain? Check. Racing heart? Check. Stomachache? She'd never had that, but suddenly her stomach lurched as she thought about it.

Cass decided to distract herself with homework. As she was reading for history, she zoned out. If she had anxiety instead of precognition, then why was her precognition right all those times, even when she wasn't working on Benson's case?

She was right about Katie Crombie getting sick. She was right about the boys who cheated. But then again, why did she get all those nervous feelings at the school dance?

Seeing Leo for the first time and her heart racing didn't coincide with anything tragic then. But maybe that was regular anxiety?

Cass sighed. If that was anxiety, it felt like it was the same as precognition. And what's to say they're two different things instead of the same?

Cass massaged her forehead as a headache started strangling her brain. To her relief, Elroy crawled out from under her bed and rubbed his head against her bedroom doorframe. He walked up to her and started meowing.

"Oh, Elroy," Cass began, getting on the floor to pet him. "I had a weird day."

The fluffy cat collapsed on his back, then showed his stomach and started purring.

"I don't know if all this stuff I did was based on my feelings and I have actual problems, or if that detective was just messing with me."

Elroy purred and tried to catch her hands as she rubbed his stomach. He lightly bit her hand and then licked it.

"Oh, sorry, kitty," she sighed. "I just don't know what's real and what's not. Also I don't want to do homework."

She kept petting him until she felt better.

✱✱✱

Cass unhurriedly walked into the locker room the next morning, trying to keep calm with all the information swimming in her head. Everything was going to be okay. Then a locker next to her slammed and she jumped a foot.

"You're not going to believe this!" Lenore said excitedly. "Sorry about that."

"What is it?"

"Betty called me back last night and apologized for being mean. Even better, she's having a little tea party Saturday and invited us. We can get to know her better—maybe sneak through their house for evidence that she killed Mr. Benson."

"Okay, but if she killed Mr. Benson, why dispose of his body in your woods?" Cass found herself suddenly asking.

"Because it wasn't near her? She could have driven quietly and dragged his body to the woods?"

"She's old and kinda skinny. How could she carry another person?"

"Maybe she's been working out? Maybe she got a friend to ask her? Why are you negating all my investigation?"

"Well, it's all kind of speculation, isn't it? Old people need help lifting heavy stuff unless they're super buff. Betty seemed innocent when we talked to her."

"Yeah, but you also told me your heart was racing when you talked to her that Sunday. That's an indicator from your psychic powers."

Some classmates turned around at the phrase "psychic powers." Both girls tried talking quietly in hushed tones.

"Psychic powers? Lenore, do you realize how ridiculous that sounds? What if I'm not psychic and it's all just anxiety?"

"Anxiety?" Lenore asked, confused. "You don't have anxiety, that's for people who are too scared to order food at a restaurant. You've picked up on so many clues from this case with your feelings and intuition. That's totally precog."

"Okay, but what about the dance?" Cass asked. "I felt anxious when I met Leo."

"Yeah, but Leo Fernandez also helped us investigate if Mr. Benson had a previous lover in Kentucky," Lenore said. "Even though it turned out to be a dud, he did x out the idea that the lover was from there."

Classmates were back to staring at the girls at the drop of Leo's name.

"Yeah, but what if that's just anxiety because he's hot and not at all related to the case? And what's to say this isn't all anxiety?" Cass said.

"What's to say it's not?" Lenore said. "When did this idea of anxiety ever come up?"

"Just something I heard about for the first time yesterday."

"From who?"

Cass stopped talking. She knew things would get worse if she mentioned him.

"From who, Cass?" Lenore pushed.

You know what? Let Lenore have it, Cass thought.

"From Detective Gomez. I met with him yesterday and told him all about our case. From how we solve cases with my precog, to those love letters. And I also gave him those love letters. He left us the copies since there's nothing else we can pick up on them. And guess what? He thinks my feelings are anxiety, which honestly match up with the internet's description."

The two minute bell went off, but all the seventh grade girls in physical education were still in the locker room.

"YOU WHAT?" Lenore screamed. "How dare you go talk to that cop after we said we weren't going to let the police win this case! Those letters were ours!"

"*We* never said that. You did!" Cass screamed back. "It's not about winning the case, it's about helping Mr. Benson. It always has been. Those were *his* letters. When did you change tunes?"

"Change tunes? When did we ever do tunes? It was always going to be us solving this despite what the authorities and adults tell us! Now you're letting some cop take over all our hard work. All your precog from stopping a murderer."

"Precog isn't real! My feelings about all this were just made-up fear crap that pushed me to do stuff. Did I ever want to do that stuff? NO! I did it based on your bad ideas. You made me do a lot of stupid crap for your fun, Lenore, but did you ever think about my feelings? How I was uncomfortable for the last few weeks interviewing these old people and asking them awkward questions? The reason I didn't go to Marnie's house the other day wasn't because I forgot. I reached her house and then I panicked. I heard voices saying not to go in. I couldn't breathe, my legs were wobbling, and I just ran off and cried. I cried because you keep making me do stupid crap I don't want to do!"

At this point, both girls were yelling over the morning Pledge of Allegiance. No one moved.

"I did not force you to do anything! Maybe if you didn't want to do what we did, you should have told me like a normal person instead of bottling it up! I didn't make you do all that stuff we did—you chose to go along with me. So stop blaming me for your problems!"

"My problem is that you're not a good friend who listens!"

"My problem is you're not a good friend who goes behind my back!"

"You know what, screw you! I don't want to be your friend!" Cass yelled with tears rolling down her face.

None of the girls in the locker room noticed Coach Webber silently walk in. He stopped and made an awkward face at all the girls watching Cass and Lenore yelling at each other.

"I don't want to be yours, either! FRIENDSHIP OVER!" Lenore yelled.

"GIRLS! PE started five minutes ago," Webber matched their voice level. "Everyone get out and do five laps for warm-ups! Fairchild! Hurley! Stop crying and yelling and give me an extra twenty push-ups for fighting."

Everyone awkwardly ran out of the locker room at the teacher's instructions. Lenore looked back at Cass who was turned away but still visibly shaken. Their friendship may have been over, but she still worried that she had irreparably damaged Cass. She left after realizing she was still in the locker room, running out as the door swished back and forth upon her exit.

Coach Webber changed to his soft voice and bent down to face Cass.

"Fairchild, I don't have daughters, I don't understand your age range and sex and what just happened, but maybe wash your face and calm down before you join the rest of class," he offered.

✳✳✳

The worst part of having most of your classes with your best friend is that you still see them all day when you are fighting. By lunch, Lenore made a beeline to her volleyball teammates. Cass went to her cross-country friends.

"Hey, are you okay," Jada asked her as she sat down. "We heard about your locker room fight with Lenore."

"Yeah, I'm fine," Cass said. "What are people saying about it?"

"Some said you guys were arguing about Leo Fernandez, and then being psychic, and then being bad friends. Someone said you cried, another said Lenore punched you and that's why you cried."

"Why is crying the focus of all these stories?"

Jada shrugged.

"Cass, we just hope you're okay. Maybe people will forget all about this by high school."

"So, people are just calling me a crier?" Cass asked her teammates.

"Yeah, and that Lenore started it," Emma Stanwell added. "But we are all curious, what's going on with you and Leo Fernandez, by the way? Why were you two talking about him? Did you both fight over him?"

Cass sighed.

"Nothing's going on there," she said. "He was trying to help me with a problem. Also, I thought it was obvious Lenore likes Noah Thompson."

Everyone at the table made an *ooh* sound and looked at each other. Cass didn't like spreading gossip but also didn't want to be the center of attention. Might as well spread it about her former friend.

Chapter Thirty-One

Cass sat down on the curb, waiting for her mom to arrive after late pickup at school. The orange setting sky reminded her of the rapid season change.

She looked to her left to see Lenore at the other end of the school, also sitting on the curb with another book in her hand. She couldn't tell if Lenore was fake reading it or just skimming.

As Cass kept an eye out for her mom's car, she was suddenly approached by Leo.

"Hey, Cass, how's it going?" he asked.

"Um, I'm guessing you didn't hear about this morning, then?" she asked. She watched some cars pull up.

"Yeah, I did, but I'm confused why Lenore would punch you over me? I thought she liked Noah."

"No, no, this is all wrong," Cass shook her head. "There was no punching, nothing was over you, and, yeah, she likes Noah."

Leo sat down at the curb with her.

"Okay, how's the case going?" he switched topics.

"You see, that's why we got in a fight," Cass started to blabber. "We don't know where it's going or anything. So, I met with the detective working on it to get some help. Of course, that's a bust and Lenore gets all mad at me because now he'll supposedly solve it before us, even though there's still barely any leads for the motive or the murderer. The worst part is I care about this case, but I think I have my limits emotionally?'

Leo looked at her, not sure how to respond.

"So, the thing about the secret lover back where the guy was from?" he asked. "What happened there?"

"I called his daughter and that was moot," she said. "Lenore and I went back and asked Marnie when Mr. Benson asked for the check, and she said it was about two years ago, dating the letters back then. We also got invited to his church friend's house for a tea party this weekend. There might be a woman there who was his lover; Lenore thinks it's this one woman. I don't think I'll go."

"Why not?"

"Lenore will be there. I don't know if I can stand to see her, let alone be in the same room as her."

"But aren't you doing the case for Mr. Benson's sake, not hers?"

Cass rolled her eyes at how this cute boy could hear the gossip but still get to the truth of what happened in the morning.

"Yeah, exactly!" she said. "That's what hurts—that now I need to solve this case, but I don't know how to do it on my own. Going to the party could be just a useless waste."

"I think you should go. You never know what you'll get. Plus, you might regret it if you don't," Leo said.

Right then Cass realized the car in front of her was her mom's van. She got up and into the car.

"So, was there a reason you took so long to get in?" her mom asked.

"Well I was talking to Leo."

"Did he ask you out? If he did, you know the dating policy your father and I set up."

"He didn't ask me out, he's just helping me with the case."

"And then he's gonna ask you out when you solve it?"
"He's not asking me out!" Cass snapped.

Chapter Thirty-Two

Betty Green was very lucky. Of all the fall weekends to hold a garden party, this one would have perfect weather. Her hedges were still green without the flowers blooming. Her tables were set up with all kinds of white lace tablecloths and doilies, all with statues of little animals in human clothes or store-bought flowers in a vase.

Betty woke up an hour before Joe and got about her routine to get the party perfectly right. She did a little yoga for strength before morning coffee. She delicately brushed her hair while deciding what to wear before settling on a green outfit that complemented her jewelry.

It had been a few bad weeks with all this murder and investigating from both the cops and the neighbor girls. Could she please have some peace for once?

Maybe if she held a little party for her fellow churchgoers, brought the girls, and then calmed them down, then everything else would go back to normal. As neighbors and church friends came in, she was calm. But when Lenore showed up alone with a dour face, wearing a blue knit dress that looked like her mom forced her in and a bundt cake in hand, she was worried.

"Nice to see you, Eleanor," Betty said as she opened her front door. "Where is Cassandra? Is she still coming?"

"I don't know, she might," Lenore said as she passed off the cake. "Which way is the party?"

"Backyard. Straight through the hall here," she guided Lenore to the back doors.

Betty sighed at the thought of only one jumpy girl at the party. Everyone could ignore Lenore, but Cass was quieter and seemed to take herself more seriously. She always expressed her emotions on her face. Without Cass, maybe no one would calm down.

She greeted Alexandra Stark and Sherri Jepsen as they entered. It looked like they were the last guests, and she went to the garden and began talking to others. As she complimented Marnie Woodson's earrings, she heard the doorbell.

To her surprise and happiness, she found Cass standing there with a nervous face, wearing a green cotton dress with leggings and sneakers, holding a chocolate bundt cake.

"Hi, Mrs. Green," Cass said. "My mom made this."

Betty took the cake.

"It's great to see you, Cassandra! Eleanor is here, too. You two can sit together."

Cass sighed.

"I don't know if I want to see her right now," she said. "Is there anyone else I can sit with?"

"Well there's not a seating chart, I just assumed you two would sit together." Betty started ringing her hands.

"Great," Cass let out another little sigh.

She followed the hostess outside to the magnificent backyard with brickwork and tall trees and hedges. A bunch of the women Cass knew waved at her. She saw Lenore stare at her and stared straight back. Lenore let go of the stare as she sat with Mrs. Stark and Mrs. Jepsen.

"Go sit anywhere Cass," Betty encouraged her. "Do you have a favorite type of tea?"

"I like the box of honey vanilla chamomile my mom buys," Cass offered.

"I'll get one of the servers to give you chamomile," she responded.

Cass kind of wandered around the back yard for a bit. Mrs. Green's backyard looked like a lush paradise. It was a mystery how she kept it so green in almost November.

"It almost looks plastic," Marnie said.

Cass turned around quickly.

"Did I scare you for a second?" Marnie said.

"Only a little." Cass gave a small laugh.

"Sorry, I'm used to living alone," Marnie laughed. "How are you doing, Cass?"

"I am alright," Cass replied.

"Do you want to sit at my table?"

"Sure," Cass smiled.

Cass followed Marnie to a table with other women who looked like they were in their fifties.

"Girls, this is Cass," Marnie began. "We live in the same neighborhood. I'm also helping her with the investigation. Cass, this is Jewel, Norah, Jane, Twyla, Catherine, and June."

All the women politely nodded and waved to Cass as she took a seat.

"So, you're doing an investigation?" Twyla asked with a smile. "What kind of investigation?"

"Do you remember old Edward Benson?" Marnie asked. "Well, Cass and one of her friends are trying to figure out who killed him almost a month ago."

"Oh, I remember him now!" June said. "He always looked like he was sleeping in church."

Everyone except Cass laughed.

"So, Cass, how is it going?" Norah asked.

"Well, we still don't have a murder suspect," Cass began. "And we don't have a good motive. Mr. Benson may have had a jealous lover, or the lover's husband may have killed him, but we don't know. We know he had floorboards to stash old letters."

Everyone laughed again.

"But I don't know, are there any older women who were sick about two years ago who recovered? That would actually help."

"Help what?" Betty suddenly asked. Cass looked up at the hostess. She stood with a server holding a teapot. He began pouring Cass her requested chamomile tea in some fancy china.

Cass ignored the nagging voices in her head as she pulled the mystery notebook from her tote bag.

"Mrs. Green, do you know anyone at your church who was ill about two years ago?"

"Pardon?"

"Was there any female churchgoer about two years ago who became suddenly ill and needed help financially?"

"Well, most women my age get sick from whatever. Anyone over sixty here has probably been ill. Why?"

Cass tried her best to look Betty in the eyes but then noticed the woman was wearing ruby earrings. Where did Cass leave Mr. Benson's secret jewelry again?

"Nice earrings," Cass said.

"Thanks, they are very precious."

"I bet. Well, I think Mr. Benson was secretly dating a married woman," Cass looked her point-blank in the eyes. "And that woman got sick with something and needed financial contributions. I kind of need to know who here was sick so I can eliminate all possible suspects."

"Why, dear? Isn't that sensitive information?"

"Everything sensitive should have been disregarded as soon as Mr. Benson was found dead in the woods."

Everyone became quiet.

"But, honey, while his death was unnatural, don't you think you two kids are taking it too far? You're worrying people about him too much."

"Maybe if people worried about Mr. Benson when he was alive, we wouldn't be here and he wouldn't be dead. Mr. Benson was a passionate man who had cares and dreams and feelings. He had love; shouldn't we solve this for love?"

All the women at the table looked from Cass to Mrs. Green. Her jaw was open.

"Yes, we all deserve love, don't we? Carry on," she briskly walked away.

All the women began cooing over Cass.

"You showed her, Nancy Drew," Marnie said.

"Nancy Drew?"

"Literary teen detective," Marnie replied. "I thought you liked to read."

"I do, I just haven't read her stuff."

"So, anyone over sixty here, hm," Twyla said. "That narrows it down to about twenty people here, but we're all just a part of the Episcopal Church. Edward Benson may have had more groups he knew."

"Oh no, my friend and I—I narrowed it down. Mr. Benson was a bit of a loner," Cass stuttered a little. "All he liked was fishing, going to church, his cats, and possibly dancing."

"Aw, can you imagine him trying to woo a woman here by dancing?" Norah said. "All of these ladies would be lucky."

Some of the group laughed.

"So, there's not a random stranger he could have dated?" Twyla asked.

"I called his daughter, and apparently he and his previous wife were attached at the hip until her death. He didn't have any older female friends reach out to him after she died."

"Well, your leads seem well thought out," Marnie said. "By the way, did you ring my doorbell the other day? Someone rang it, but when I got to the door no one was there. I thought maybe you wanted to talk some more when your friend Lenore called me."

"I was passing by your house, but I didn't ring," Cass lied. "It was probably a neighbor kid. Excuse me, I have to go to the bathroom."

Cass got up out of anxiety and made a beeline to the Green house. Unfortunately, there was a line at the downstairs bathroom. Feeling self-conscious, Cass decided to break another house rule—marked by a little red string on the stairs, indicating no one was to go up—and went upstairs to the second-floor bathroom.

✳✳✳

Lenore felt terrible fighting with Cass. Her friend was right—she overpowered often, and she wanted to make it up. She wasn't sure how to act at this party so she stayed with her neighbors, both wearing long clothing for an unusually sunny day. Mrs. Stark was chatty as usual, but Mrs. Jepsen almost seemed to keep a tight lip.

"Why isn't your friend Cass sitting with us?" Mrs. Stark asked.

"It's a long story," Lenore said. "But how are you two doing?"

"I'm great. My husband and I had a blast going to bingo this week, and the service today hit right at home," Mrs. Stark smiled.

"I'm alright," Mrs. Jepsen said as she sipped her tea.

"So, um, why is this party happening, really?" Lenore leaned in to ask. "Because it seems these are only the women at your church, and then Cass and me. Is this related to the murder of Mr. Benson?"

Both women stared at her.

"I think it is, and I think Mrs. Green wants everyone to be calm about it," Mrs. Stark leaned in.

"Pah, what a weak idea," Mrs. Jepsen said. "Only *she* keeps worrying about this murder."

"And why's that?" Lenore said.

"No one seems down at church; I think we've moved on,"

Mrs. Jepsen said.

"How's everything going?" Mrs. Green interrupted them. Lenore looked to her.

"Good," she said.

"And how's the solving of the case?"

"It is as it is," Lenore shrugged.

Mrs. Green started asking the other women at the table questions—during which Lenore tried to make eye contact with Cass, who was out of her seat. At some point, Mrs. Green broke her train of thought by touching her, asking if she needed anything. Lenore remembered staring at the woman's scarlet outfit and recognized her familiar jewelry. Was she wearing real rubies?

✳✳✳

After washing her hands in peace, Cass heard some chatter coming from the main bedroom and couldn't help herself from eavesdropping. She stayed in the bathroom with the door open.

"I wanted this party to go right, you know? I've been having a hard time keeping up my charade," she heard Mrs. Green say.

"I know, I know, but you're strong, and you'll get through it," she heard Sherri Jepsen say. "But living with Joe can't be that bad if you're not seeing the other man now."

Cass held back a gasp.

"But I miss him so much. Joe never provided for me much after my stroke."

"But Joe is your husband, and at this point it really is 'til death do us part."

"It's just getting harder everyday," Mrs. Green said.

"Yeah, but you're so strong."

"Sometimes I wish I could take our car and drive away silently into the night. It wouldn't be hard."

"But what about your life here? What about all that mess you made last month that Joe helped you through? He wasn't even mad."

"I know, you're right. You're right. I guess we should get back to the party."

Cass closed the bathroom door and waited for the sounds of the feet going downstairs. She heard one set go down, then waited a minute before hearing another set leave before flushing the toilet and running the sink. She snuck back down.

Mrs. Green was having an affair and crap went down a month ago. She *had* to be the murderer. She had to. Cass' first instinct was to grab Lenore and tell her, but they weren't on speaking terms. *Screw it.*

Cass made a beeline to get out of the house and back to the party to find Lenore. She got outside to see her table waving at her but tried turning around to find her former friend. Lenore seemed to have disappeared.

Mrs. Stark waved as she was passing by. Cass grabbed her arm.

"Mrs. Stark, where's Lenore?"

"She went home fifteen minutes ago, dear," she replied. "She said she needed to finish studying for a vocabulary test."

Cass sighed at her friend's leaving but wasn't surprised Lenore would quit something once it got boring. She went back to her table.

"Welcome back," Twyla smiled.

Cass ended up cleaning as she waited for her parents to pick her up at the end of the party. She picked up the folding chairs to put on the side of the house. As she finished hanging them back up on the rack Mrs. Green was renting, she was amazed at the sight of Mrs. Jepsen holding four chairs.

"Mrs. Jepsen, you don't need to do that, I can finish carrying chairs," Cass said.

"Oh, no worries, dear! My SilverSneakers class is paying off," Mrs. Jepsen replied. "So, how is your murder investigation going?"

"Really good, I think."

"Yeah?" she nodded gingerly. "Any breakthroughs?"

"I think so."

"Well, that's good. Hopefully we can put this past us."

Right then Cass' phone pinged with her mom's text saying she was parked at the front of the house. Cass tried scurrying away quickly, but Mrs. Green called her name. She was washing utensils in the kitchen, cleaning a large cake knife.

"Miss Cassandra, going already? Thanks for helping clean up."

"Yes ma'am. It was no problem"

"Did you have fun?"

"Yep."

"Hopefully you are going to put all this murder behind you now," she said as she dried the knife with a towel.

"Sure."

Cass hurried out the front door and jumped into her mom's minivan.

She answered "fine" to every one of her mom's questions as they went home. Through the front door, she ran to her room and took some deep breaths.

It's okay. You're safe now, Cass kept thinking. *There wasn't any danger. You're safe from Mrs. Green,* her thoughts raced. Cass tried to pick up her phone but her hands were shaking from nerves. Why was she feeling so bad at a time like this?

She tried to distract herself from the excitement by reading an adventure book for a bit, but that did nothing. Cass' thoughts kept going back to Mrs. Green. The woman basically killed Mr. Benson a month ago and lied to poor Joe about it all. If they had a quiet car, they must have taken it to dump the body. She was able to lift some heavy teapots and cakes, so she wasn't worried about weight lifting a dead body anymore.

Cass went back to her dresser drawer to see if the rubies were there. Her arms were shaking the entire five-second journey to the furniture. She grew more and more nervous as she moved her hand around the drawer and did not pick up anything. What happened to the rubies?

Oh yeah, she showed them to Mrs. Jepsen and Mrs. Green at the open house before getting roped in to meeting Kevin Scarpino. Mrs. Green mentioned something about an affair and that she liked the jewelry. She must have taken them home!

She tried to journal in the mystery notebook, but her handwriting was basically scribbles. She couldn't take it anymore. Fingers and arms as wobbly as spaghetti, she attempted to grab her phone. Finally, she grabbed hold and scrolled through her contacts. After several minutes, she was able to get Detective Gomez's number.

✳✳✳

Detective Gomez woke up at six a.m. Monday and checked his personal phone: No new emails—thank goodness—a few texts from his family's group chat on what they were bringing to Thanksgiving, and a few notifications on his private Instagram. All good there. He got dressed for the day and made cereal at his table. He turned on his work phone: one voicemail from Cass and a few texts from her saying, "please text me back."

He tried listening to the voicemail but couldn't make out what the twelve-year-old was saying. She spoke nervously, quickly, and almost sounded like she was going to burst into tears. Probably something about the murder.

He finished his cereal, brushed his teeth, and drove to the police department. Gomez nodded and smiled at his fellow detectives and hadn't even put down his phones when Sergeant Fuller called him into his office.

"Detective Gomez," the sergeant said.

"Sir."

"Did you get any messages on your work phone recently?"

"Yeah, Cass Fairchild called me, but I couldn't make out what she said."

"Okay, because she also called the police department last night and said she found out who the murderer was. Betty Green. She apparently went to church with Edward Benson. The girl said she overheard Green admit she was having an affair and caused a big mess about a month ago. Dispatchers sent police out there and found old letters corresponding to the ones you got the other week. The FBI is checking the letters for handwriting, and we have her in custody. Go question her."

"Yes, sir."

CHAPTER THIRTY-THREE

"Everything's okay," Cass said to herself.

BaDUM. "Everything's okay." *BaDUM.* "Everything's okay." *BaDUM.* "Everything's o–"

"Miss Fairchild," Mrs. Leary snarled.

Cass looked up, shaken out of her trance. Everyone in English class was staring at her.

"I'm sorry?"

"Miss Fairchild, read the next line."

"Oh," she said. She guessed where they were in *The Outsiders* and read the next few paragraphs as everyone went back to looking at their own copies. Mrs. Leary eventually passed the next reading to Alexis Crafts. As her classmate read aloud, Cass caught Lenore staring at her. Cass shrugged back. She wasn't quite ready to talk to Lenore.

Cass was still reeling from calling the police department that morning. The sergeant she spoke to said they would handle it and thanked her.

But this was more than thinking about a murderess getting caught. This was risking detention—Cass was carrying her phone on her hoping to get a news alert about the murder. Mrs. Leary thankfully didn't look into her binder to see her phone there hiding in plain sight. But everything was okay for now. No phone was caught, and no news didn't mean it wasn't going to hit the presses.

After class, Cass outpaced the rest of the girls in winter conditioning for track and field. She knew the police weren't going to tell her anything, but hopefully the news stations were polishing their reports as she continued her day.

After practice, she scarfed down dinner and finished her homework half-heartedly. She bounded down the stairs while her dad was watching the national game shows that played before prime time. She sighed, a little out of breath as she plopped down on the couch.

"What's the rush?" her father asked. "*Greendale* isn't on tonight is it?"

"I want to catch the news," she said.

"The news? What twelve-year-old girl likes watching the news?" her mom asked as she sat next to her.

"I think the case I worked on was solved."

"Okay, let us know when it starts," she said.

Cass got up from the couch and went back to brooding over the day at the family computer, constantly checking the local paper's website to see if they published anything. Finally, she sat down with her parents and watched their police procedural drama after 9:30. At ten, the news came on. Cass sat upright and grabbed a couch pillow as her heart raced.

"Tonight," an overdressed man said, "A woman confesses to murdering an old neighbor, student loans are on the rise, and what to expect for the weekend's high school football playoffs. All on WQTL 32."

Betty Green's mugshot flashed on the screen. Cass leaned forward as her mom gasped.

"Was that the woman whose party you were just at—" her mom was cut off by Cass shushing.

"Today 73-year-old Moon Town woman Betty Green

admitted to murdering Edward Benson and leaving his body in the woods over a month ago," a young reporter holding a microphone said. It was obvious the news had filmed the segment earlier in the day as it was daylight outside the police department as she spoke. "According to a press release from the Moon Town PD, old love letters corresponding with evidence obtained by police were found in her house. Nothing further was released, but the statement thanked all witnesses involved who helped solve the case. This is Leann Jacobs reporting."

The camera switched to two anchors who switched to talking about the most effective ways to get rid of bed bugs.

Cass was silent with her parents. She felt the silence around her. All that work, all that sneaking around, all those anxiety dreams.

"That's it?" she asked.

"I guess so," her dad said as he grabbed the remote. "Bedtime?"

"But what about how the case was solved, or how it was discovered Betty was having an affair? Anything more about the love letters? What's the total motive? I did not check my phone throughout the day, risking detention, so I could get this tiny news report! Lenore and I broke up our friendship because of this!"

"Cassandra Felicity, you did what today?" her dad said sternly.

"Babe, Cass's been through a lot," her mom said. "Want to talk about it?"

Cass grabbed her phone to look up the newspaper's coverage of events. They basically regurgitated what the news report said.

"Talk about it? I want to RAGE ABOUT IT!"

"Can you do it without waking either of your siblings?" her mom said.

Cass took a deep breath. But she felt like she wanted to cry. What was this feeling? Crying and mad?

"I have—" she said between sobs, "had nightmares about Mr.

Benson's death," she sobbed some more. "I have heard him telling me to finish—" she sobbed. Her mom handed her a tissue box. "Finish this. Lenore and I got into a fight over all of this. We wrote a mystery notebook, investigated cranky people," she felt hot tears, "had a c-list celebrity distract us from the murder, and all we learned from TV is basically the evidence was literally right under a bed. Nothing there. No motive—that's it."

Cass began punching the pillow she was holding. Her parents looked uneasy at each other before turning back to her.

"Honey, you've had nightmares?" her dad said. "Are you sleeping okay?"

"Yeah," Cass said. She realized she was opening herself up to prodding by her parents. Maybe she didn't have precognition, but she didn't want to get into all of this at the moment. "Just with this murder you know? It's a lot to handle. I just have a lot of feelings."

"Why don't you write them out?" her mom suggested. "Go use the desktop."

Cass walked to the front room with the family computer and pressed a little too hard on the Word app. She eviscerated her anger of the police handling of all of this after she trusted them; she typed her hurt at the news' handling of the arrest; she furiously let out all the pain she felt from her feelings through the whole case. Nothing was her reward. She kept pounding the keys until her fingers hurt.

Her mom slipped into the room and hugged her from behind the chair.

"It's okay, honey, it really is," she said.

Cass tried to say something, but nothing was coming out.

"The news does that to people, but you know what? Maybe we should do our own thing to celebrate the end of this case."

Cass nodded at the suggestion as she deleted the two thousand word ramble.

"We can go out and get dinner, wherever you want, maybe this Friday. You can tell us all about the hardships you faced. We can invite anyone, if you want? How about that?"

She nodded as she sobbed into her mother's shoulders.

Cass was surprised that she was able to fall asleep quickly that night. She awoke in the same gray woods she'd been dreaming of since Mr. Benson's death. Everything seemed to be in black and white except for herself. She looked below to see the dead man, but his body was covered in frozen leaves. His face was now covered. She tried getting on her knees to talk to him, but she heard nothing.

Cass tried scraping the leaves off of the body. She uncovered his face, but it was lifeless. She tried putting her ear against his mouth. No sign of breathing, no noise. He was as still as the day she found his body in real life.

Cass walked away from the body. She wanted to stop, but her legs kept wandering aimlessly through the forest.

Chapter Thirty-Four

Cass didn't jump this time when she heard Lenore's voice behind her gym locker.

"I guess the case is solved," Lenore said softly.

"I guess so," Cass said shortly.

"What tipped you off that Mrs. Green was the murderer?"

"Overheard Mrs. Green tell Mrs. Jepsen she was having an affair and did something bad about a month ago. The police did the rest."

"Did you notice she was wearing ruby earrings like the ones we discovered? I got suspicious and wanted to dig deeper, but my mom made me go home early."

"Well, the earrings I discovered, but yeah, that was also kind of obvious. She must have stolen them when Kevin Scarpino distracted me."

"Why are you being like this?"

"Like what?"

"Why are you being mean to me, Cass Felicity Fairchild! I'm trying to be friends with you again. I miss you! And also I think something's not right with the case."

"Well, you said our friendship is over, and now I'm speaking up," Cass spoke with a chill in her voice. "Also, what's there left with the case? The police found a corresponding love letter to the ones we found."

"But we don't know whose letter that really is until the FBI looks into it! It takes a while to identify. Also, the two didn't run in any similar circles."

Cass closed her locker.

"Lenore, the police solved everything. Betty admitted to it. The handwriting will come back. She wore the rubies. It's all over. Just move on." She left the locker room.

Cass wasn't ready to make nice with Lenore. Maybe it was because she felt Lenore was a bad friend. Maybe it was because she solved the case without her. Maybe it was because she also didn't feel right about the outcome of it all but didn't want to admit it.

✳✳✳

Cass walked toward the girls locker room that afternoon. Leo poked his head out of a math classroom as she passed by.

"Hey, Cass!" he exclaimed.

"Heeeey," she said, trying to not make her voice go high. Her heart started racing. "What are you doing after school? Detention?"

"Nope, I'm waiting for the engineering club to start soon. You?"

"Winter conditioning for track."

"Are you good at running?"

"I think so, but I'm not the best." Cass paused awkwardly.

The two stood in silence for a few seconds.

"I saw the news that the police arrested the killer from that case you were working on," he said as he pushed back his hair. "Did you solve it?"

"Yeah, I think I did."

"So, you didn't solve it?"

"Well, the handwriting needs to come back as Mr. Benson's and Mrs. Green's," Cass began. "But Mrs. Green apparently confessed to it all. And I overheard her say she was having an affair. There was a mess of some sort about a month ago, and I saw her wearing the same ruby earrings I found at the house."

"So, then you solved it."

"Yeah, but something doesn't feel right."

"Like what?'

Cass approached Leo, standing a foot away from him.

"Usually when I solve cases with Lenore, we have people confess to us. It's not all done by police. Also, it was weird how there weren't any statements from the police in that press release. I just feel like we're missing something. Maybe it's knowing her motivation to kill Mr. Benson."

"That could come out later on, maybe at the trial," he said. "So, what do you guys do when you solve cases?"

"Usually we write down the conclusion in our notebook and then get smoothies at The Roast of Moon Town," she said. "But this was a one-woman job."

"Well, what are you doing then? Smoothies for one?"

"Actually, my mom is taking my family out to Beijing Gardens on Friday," Cass' heart raced as the next few words escaped her mouth. "My mom said I could bring friends if I wanted. Want to join?"

"I'll have to ask my family what I'm doing this weekend, but that'd be fun," he said. "Is anyone else going?"

"Hopefully Lenore," Cass blurted out.

"Nice. Sounds like you two made up." He then started talking about getting in contact for the weekend. Cass felt a surge of euphoria and fear at the same time. It was like she was at the dance again.

Cass was distracted by Leo's dark eyes and bright smile; she didn't hear what he said.

"Your phone?" he asked again. "Are you going to take out your phone so you can add my number?"

"Oh yeah!" Cass said a little loudly. She grabbed her cell phone to exchange details. After getting his number, she walked a little faster to the girls locker room.

Cass kept staring at the text from Leo that night. All it said was "hi, it's Leo," but that was enough for her.

As the week passed, she felt less irritated by Lenore, but her former friend's eagerness to make up made her more annoyed. She wanted space. Cass was glad Lenore didn't have a phone because she knew she'd get a flood of "hi," "how's it going," or "I'm sorry" texts regularly.

During Mrs. Leary's class one day, they had the writing prompt "like sidewalk chalk during the rain, his dreams washed away." Lenore volunteered to read her story out loud. It was about a man who gave up his friends for fame and realizing the former was more important. She then added an epilogue about the man feeling so sorry and asking for forgiveness. The friends all then went and got coffee and had a dance party. The other kids laughed at the story, but Cass rolled her eyes.

Yet again, Leo confirmed he was going to dinner with her, so Cass needed to pass along the invite to save face. Even if she said Lenore couldn't make it, her family would needle Leo at dinner. She lazily emailed Lenore Thursday about the event.

"YES! MOM SAID YES. WILL BE THERE!" Lenore emailed back within two minutes. Cass wondered why she was typing in all caps but sighed and moved on.

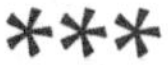

That Friday, Cass dressed up for the dinner with a green blouse with puffy sleeves. She recreated the braided bun style Mrs. Hurley gave her for the dance to look cute for Leo. He and

Lenore were also dressed up as if ready to go to a dance as well, talking casually outside the restaurant as Cass' family pulled up. Her heart raced at the sight of them both—nerves of excitement for Leo and nerves of retribution from Lenore.

It's okay, it's okay, it's okay, she kept telling herself.

She tried to casually approach both of them, but Lenore's "here's your crush" funny face distracted her. Cass almost gagged.

"Hey," Leo said.

"Hi," Lenore exclaimed.

"Guys!" she said. *Guys? What kind of greeting is that?*

Cass felt like turning into a little ball as her parents greeted her crush. They both were trying to be cool, but with baby Lucy drooling all over her stroller, it was hard to pay attention to them. Tommy also played one hundred questions with Leo, asking who he was, why he was there, did he really like Chinese food, and how they met.

Cass tried to sit between Leo and Tommy when they finally got a table but Lenore kicked the latter out to get close to her friend. The middle schoolers faced the restaurant wall as Tommy and her parents faced the window, with Lucy's high chair at the north end by her mom.

Cass zoned out as her parents tried to get to know Leo and asked Lenore to catch them up with her life. Leo was also asking questions about Lucy—she kept waving at him and strangers through the restaurant. The waiters came and went with drinks, and everyone debated what to order.

Cass was content. She looked at her parents, her crush, and her sort-of-friend and was glad they were able to celebrate. As she was looking around, she noticed the Jepsens sit in a booth across from her. They waved to her and Lenore and went back to their menus.

Cass got halfway through her meal when she had to use the restroom. While she washed her hands at the bathroom sink, Mrs. Jepsen walked in and came up to the bathroom mirror.

"Hey, Mrs. Jepsen, how are you?" Cass smiled.

"I'm good, dear, just out with my husband. Celebrating being two years cancer-free," the woman started fingering her hair.

"Congrats," Cass smiled.

Cass looked into the mirror and noticed Mrs. Jepsen wearing the same ruby earrings and the matching necklace as Mrs. Green.

"Hey, I like your earrings. Did you get them from Mrs. Green?"

"Betty? Pah, no. She borrowed them from me. They're quite rare and special to me. Glad I got them back from that weak-minded woman before she was arrested."

Cass' heart started beating out of her chest.

"So, 'rare,' as in they're not something you can find at a mall?"

"Exactly," Mrs. Jepsen said. "Someone very special gave them to me while I was suffering."

"Mr. Jepsen?" Cass squeaked.

Mrs. Jepsen paused, then pulled lipstick out of her purse and started applying it.

"I wish," she said.

Cass tried her best to speak as slowly as possible, her heart pounding at the sight of the same shade of lipstick she had found in Mr. Benson's house. Her right arm felt as if someone had dropped an anvil on it. She tried to massage it casually.

"So, was cancer expensive?"

Mrs. Jepsen laughed quietly. "Is a $2.5 million mansion expensive?" she replied.

Cass found herself blocking the bathroom door. She suddenly noticed the little tears in Mrs. Jepsen's sweater as if they were pricked by rose bushes.

"How are your roses going?"

"Well, there's not much to do now," Mrs. Jepsen said. "If you're looking at my sweater, sometimes passing through the garden gets you caught."

Cass had a sudden vision of the woman trying to drag Mr.

Benson's body through the rose garden path to the woods.

"Do you like to drink vodka?" Cass blurted out.

"Why? Is something going on?"

"Ruby?" she said with tears in her eyes.

Mrs. Jepsen's eyes dilated. "What did you call me?" she seemed lost for words. "How?"

Cass dashed out of the bathroom, tears streaming down her face. She somehow overshot her table and was suddenly running outside. Her heart was pounding as if someone was playing piano on it. Her thoughts told her to *run, run, run, you're wrong, you're wrong, you're wrong, you're wrong, you're wrong, you're wrong, you're wrong*. All the thoughts were coursing through her as her heartbeat thundered in her chest. *BaDUM.BaDUM. BaDUM. BaDUM.BaDUM.BaDUM. BaDUM. BaDUM. BaDUM.BaDUM. BaDUM. BaDUM.* She couldn't run anymore. All her thoughts were back to her heartbeat going faster than it ever had before. *BaDUM.BaDUM. BaDUM. BaDUM. BaDUM.BaDUM. BaDUM. BaDUM.* She looked around, her vision completely blurred.

"Cass?" someone said. She couldn't tell if that was her mom or Lenore.

She tried turning around, but everything went black.

Chapter Thirty-Five

The window collected small rain drops against it as the drizzle started. Chicken soup scented the kitchen as Sherri Jepsen began cutting carrots and other vegetables to add to the pot as she waited. He'd be home any minute now.

Clink.

She ignored the sound hitting her kitchen door's window and turned up her kitchen radio.

Clink.

She tried to ignore it again by softly humming to the tunes.

Clink.

She finished chopping a carrot and looked out the window. Edward Benson was throwing coffee beans at the door again. She sighed, wiping her hands on her apron before opening the door.

"Edward," she said politely.

"Sherri!" he exclaimed as he hugged her. She gently put her hands around him and broke away quickly. He followed her into the kitchen as she walked back to her countertop.

"John will be getting here soon," she said as she got back to cutting.

"I don't care about John, let's get out of here like we said so many times before," Edward grabbed her left hand. She stopped cutting. "You and me, like you always said. Now's the time. I'm all packed at my house. Leave a note saying you're not sorry and let's go."

Sherri kept her gaze downward and eventually continued her chopping.

"I'm not going. Not tonight."

"But you told me we would leave," he insisted.

"Yes. But not tonight."

"Why not?" he grabbed her hand again.

"Because I have to take care of John, okay!" She released his grip and started slicing celery for the soup. "He could get ill at any moment. He stayed with me through all of this. I have to."

"But what about us? You promised me you would leave him as soon as you were healthy again and all the grandkids were married, and we would be together finally. And Rachel finally got married two weeks ago."

"I know, but I don't know if I can do it now," she said. "Please go, John is going to be home soon."

"C'mon my Ruby, you know what you need to do." He kissed her. "Let's get this show on the road."

"No!"

"Ruby, c'mon. Let's go."

"Don't call me that!" she yelled as she turned around.

"I can call you what I want! It's us together, like you said."

He tried to grab her but she slipped away. She heard a car pulling up.

"Go away!"

"No, come with me! You deserve better! Choose to be with me and let's get going! You know the dud doesn't care about you—even now when you're healthy."

Sherri was furious. He wasn't driving her to all her scans and doctor appointments. He wasn't holding her hand at the breast cancer patient support group meetings. He paid for her clinical treatment that saved her, but he ultimately wasn't the one to take her in sickness and health. Her illness made a one-eighty when John stepped up for her. John was there more than only three hours a week. John cracked jokes to make her stop worrying about the cancer coming back.

"Don't you dare say that about him! Take it back!" Sherri white knuckled her knife.

"No!" Edward stood his ground. "He's an inattentive buffoon, and you can do better with me! He's a sad dud losing his mind! He's not worthy of your love."

"Take it back!"

"No, I will never take it back! Let's go, Ruby!"

"Stop calling me that!"

"RUBY! RUBY! RUBY! RUB—" he stopped when he found a knife suddenly in his stomach. He instinctively went to cover the wound, but Sherri pulled it out, then kept stabbing.

Sherri felt her rage bloom every time she pushed the knife in. Edward tried to stop her by putting his hands over his wounds but even they got cut up. He tried to reach her wrist holding the knife, but she was much stronger thanks to her SilverSneakers classes. She had begun ignoring him for those classes with her husband.

Sherri was terrified as she stabbed him. He crumpled over. Tears streaked his cheeks as he gasped for breath until he went suddenly quiet.

Sherri stopped, breathing out. What had come over her? She screamed as the knife dropped to the floor.

All that time she spent with Edward flashed by her.

Three years ago, she was bored of the same thing with John every day. He was happy serving the community, but she felt like she was sitting around waiting to die. She really only had her gardening.

When Mr. Benson moved nearby, something bloomed in her. She had met him at The Roast of Moon Town as she was having a quiet Sunday afternoon, herself. They both reached for the same black coffee. The awkward encounter turned to laughter, which turned to talking about their lives and their families.

She sympathized with having strained relationships with children. It was difficult talking to them. He liked it when she talked about gardening, and she suddenly found herself growing roses for him.

Before she knew it, her favorite part of the week was when John left to volunteer Sundays and Edward would come over. He was a fun guy who would sometimes let loose with bad habits, like sneaking a little bottle of alcohol into his drink or smoking a cigarette—nothing John would tolerate.

She, on occasion, would go to his house and was smitten by his cats. The two boys loved her endlessly, which she appreciated since John was allergic to pets. That's why they got the macaw to keep them company, but it really annoyed her and aided in building resentment in their marriage.

Every time Edward came over, she would hide the bird upstairs so it wouldn't repeat their conversations.

Everything was great. They were sharing everything on weekends.

He would walk through the woods and sneak to the back of the house, pelting coffee beans at the window to let her know he was there on Sundays.

Sherri was most surprised the day he gave her a gift of nice rubies. Edward mentioned something about getting them at a pawn shop, but she didn't mind. She'd always wanted a nice jewelry set after being so fiscally conservative with John. He didn't even notice her jewels until a month before the murder.

"They're from Gina," she lied. "Remember, she gave them to me for my birthday a few years ago?"

"Okay," John accepted.

The secret lovers were hoping and waiting to run away one day, after her grandchildren married and all of the house was paid off.

Everything was great until she fell down the stairs. Nothing felt broken, but John insisted she go to the hospital. From there, she was diagnosed with breast cancer.

She was worried she'd be so sick that their visits would stop. But one day she found a letter under the outdoor bench.

She was happily surprised to find Mr. Benson wrote to her. So she wrote back, leaving her reply on the same bench. Writing started to get her through the treatments. They used code names; she loved being his Ruby.

Things got hard, and her doctors started suggesting experimental treatment. It was so expensive, though, and they were two hundred dollars short. But Edward—he didn't hesitate. The day after her letter complaining about treatments and insurance was placed on the bench, she had a new letter waiting with the exact amount of money she needed.

Sherri was taken aback. Not only by Edward's generosity—as soon as the treatments began, John started to step up in her care. The only way out was through, and Sherri's cancer cells were gone after four months. She was happy to recover and be taken care of by John, who was paying more attention to her, taking her to survivor meetings and extra hospital scans every few months. At first, it was hard to see Edward again when her husband was wanting to spend time with her. She kept waiting until he grew bored with her again.

Finally, a month before all of this, John was gone for a weekend fishing trip and she was free to see Edward. She snuck out of the house. It felt like she could escape. They spent the weekend at his house together. She almost forgot to leave in time to make it back before her husband.

Of course, it was that morning over coffee she told Edward to get ready to run away. Soon. He smiled at the suggestion and said he couldn't wait.

And couldn't wait, he meant. Every night he was trying to run away with her. But she wasn't ready. Not yet, anyways. It dragged on and on and annoyed her as much as John's attention since she had recovered. She didn't know if she'd ever run away with him.

Now here he was, lying in a pool of blood on her kitchen floor. She stared at his body wondering how she could have done this. Right then, the garage door opened and John came in.

"Sherri, are you alright," the old man asked.

She stayed quiet, still processing it all. He finally walked close enough to see Mr. Benson's body lying lifeless on the white tile floor. He stared at the body and then her.

"What happened, Sherri?"

She burst into tears.

"I don't know," she said. "He just came in and started threatening me and said he wanted to take me from you. He wouldn't stop grabbing me, so I stabbed him!"

"So many times?"

"I was scared!"

"What do we do?"

"I don't know. Do you think I'll get arrested for self-defense?"

"Will the jury believe you?" John worried.

"Will anyone?" she cried.

They both stood in silence.

"I got an idea," John said. "First, clean that knife."

Sherri picked up on his thoughts and ran it through the dishwasher. She pulled out the bleach from under the sink and remembered where the mop was placed. But first, she grabbed two sets of clean dishwashing gloves for them. She found some small flashlights from their closet to keep in their coats. She held Mr. Benson's ankles and he grabbed the man's shoulders. They wandered through the forest for forty-five minutes before finding a quiet area surrounded by trees where no one could find him, and laid down his body in the steady falling rain. They quietly kicked leaves around to hide their path and pulled out their flashlights to head home.

Chapter Thirty-Six

Well, this was not how she'd planned to apologize. Lenore sat in the hospital room, zoning out as Cass laid unconscious in a bed with wires attached to her.

Maybe if she'd paid more attention to Cass, the case would have been solved without her friend having a massive anxiety attack and passing out in a restaurant parking lot.

Thinking about her friend's panic attack made her realize something—precognition or not, Cass never freaked out unless something was really, really wrong.

Lenore closed her eyes to take herself back to Mrs. Green's garden party. She had looked up at the old woman and saw her wearing the *exact* jewels from Mr. Benson's bathroom. Well, that's pretty much a nail in the coffin.

Lenore then thought about Mrs. Green's behavior at the party. She wasn't carrying any chairs and had hired servants handle the cakes and tea pots. Could a stroke survivor carry a body from her side of the neighborhood to Benson's side of the woods? That didn't seem right.

She knew something was off with the case. Mrs. Green had a stroke years ago, and Mr. Benson asked for two hundred dollars two years ago. The timelines were similar, but not necessarily the same event, the more she thought of it.

Someone was framing Mrs. Green. Granted, she'd confessed. *False confessions happen all the time due to suspects feeling pressured,* Lenore thought.

But if Mrs. Green wasn't the killer, who was? And who framed her?

Lenore closed her eyes, trying to remember the scene when Cass fled the restaurant. It was like she was chasing her feelings. Wait, who told her that again?

"You look constipated when you do that."

Lenore opened her eyes. Cass was conscious again and staring back.

"Cass! You're awake!" Lenore jumped up and awkwardly hugged her friend in her hospital bed.

"Where am I?" she looked around. "What day is it?"

"St. Dymphna's, still Friday, but it's 10 p.m.," Lenore said as she checked her watch. "You passed out."

"That… makes sense," Cass said with some self-loathing. "Where's my family?"

"Your mom is home with your siblings, and your dad is talking to some doctors about your symptoms."

"Oh, okay," Cass smiled.

She was fine until she remembered Leo was at the restaurant when she had a massive panic attack. Oh gosh, he was either going to run away from her or join forces with the gossips and spread rumors. Cass lolled her head back.

"Leo's parents picked him up after the ambulance arrived," Lenore said, as if reading her mind. "No, he doesn't think you're weird. But he told me to tell you to text him when you were conscious, which I guess is now."

She handed Cass back her phone from her purse. Cass stared at her phone for a few seconds, not sure what to type.

"So, what should I text? 'Hey I'm okay?' Is that too short?" Cass asked.

"I mean, it gets the point across," Lenore replied.

"Maybe, 'Hey I'm okay, thanks for being concerned,' or is that overdoing it with guys?"

"I mean, it's not like you're asking him out while saying you're okay. You don't need to tell him you're in a hospital and your heart rate is being super monitored."

"Super monitored?"

Cass tried moving her upper body when she felt a bunch of wires attached to her chest. At least she had a hospital gown over it all.

"You weren't here for that were you?"

"I was in the hall. I told my parents to pick me up when you were conscious again."

"Why?"

"Because we're friends," Lenore said. "I know we said mean things to each other, and I'm sorry. I'll do my best to pay more attention to you and listen to what you have to say. But also, you need to speak up if you're upset. So anyways, I hope we're still friends, or I'll have to give back this friendship bracelet on my wrist."

"Keep the friendship bracelet, Hurley. I guess you're alright," Cass smiled. "I'm sorry too. I think we should get back to the case like you said."

Right then, Cass' father and a tall doctor with a stern face, round glasses, and brushed back brown hair entered the room.

"Well, she's awake and I have news to deliver, so can the other runt get out?" the stranger said. "HIPAA laws and all that."

"You make a wonderful pediatrician!" Lenore said, sarcastically. Mr. Fairchild helped her out of her chair, and she walked out of the room to call her parents.

"Miss Fairchild, I am Doctor Gary Black," he said. "What you experienced today was a major panic attack. At some point your heart rate was over three hundred beats per minute. We set you up with an EKG to monitor your heart."

Cass suddenly noticed her heart racing, immediately feeling

awkward that the machines hooked up next to her were beeping.

"We think you have generalized anxiety disorder, do you know what that is?" the doctor continued.

"Is it the thing where my heart starts racing out of nowhere and I can't help but have thoughts of the world ending?" Cass said.

"Exactly," he said. "Will you fill out this screening form for us?"

Dr. Black handed her a clipboard with a two-sided paper on it. One asked if she ever felt like nothing and if she ever had suicidal thoughts. *Nope.* She looked at the other side, which asked her about being on edge, struggling to sleep, muscle tension, and excessive worry. *Yep, yep, yes, and yep.* She handed the finished form back to the doctor who looked at it for a minute.

"Well, you're empty on the depression side," he said. "But you lit up all the marks for anxiety."

At this point, Cass was happy to have someone confirm what she was thinking. Her dad looked a little surprised.

"Honey, do you really feel these things?" her dad asked.

"Yes," Cass replied.

"Why didn't you tell your mother and I?"

"Well, you're always busy, the both of you, and I figured it was–" she cut herself off. No way was she going to tell two doctors about precog. She was young, but she didn't want to feel stupid. "It was probably nothing."

"Well, I'm going to order a heart monitor for you to wear for a week and write a referral for therapy," Dr. Black said. He then left.

"Do you want to get some rest?" her dad asked.

"No, I just realized I forgot to tell Lenore!" Cass exclaimed.

"What is it?"

"I realized who the real murderer is," Cass said. "Mrs. Green falsely confessed. It was really Mrs. Jepsen. I need to tell her and Detective Gomez before, I don't know, she flees the country or something."

Cass tried getting out of bed, but her father gently grabbed her shoulders and pushed her back.

"No, no, no, no, no," her dad said. "You passed out tonight. You're not doing anything else."

"But Dad, we got the wrong person in jail!"

"Honey, you've had a long night. The murder mystery resolution can wait until the morning!"

"But, Dad!"

"No 'buts,' Cassandra Felicity Fairchild," he said sternly. "Tonight, you are going to rest. You can resume whatever foolishness this is tomorrow. Good night."

He kissed her on the forehead and turned off the light in her hospital room. Cass laid back, sighing at all the truth bombs she had faced since dinner. Sleep was not going to come tonight.

Chapter Thirty-Seven

New mission: Get discharged as soon as possible. Cass thoughtfully answered every question the staff asked her the next morning in hopes of getting out sooner. She grimaced as the sticky pads and wires were taken off her chest and reapplied with a new heart monitor. She dressed faster than she ever thought she could.

Her dad wheeled her out to the front of the hospital as her mom was pulling up to take her home. He was staying for a shift.

Cass remembered she'd forgotten to text Leo. She was also supposed to remember to tell someone something else… She pulled up her phone to see a text from Leo from earlier, asking if she was okay.

Cass sent a message back. "I'm okay. Leaving the hospital now"

Wait, wasn't she *not* going to tell him she went to the hospital? Should she tell him she solved the murder for real this time?

Holy Crap, she forgot to tell Lenore! That's what she's forgotten. She tried calling her best friend's home phone just as she and her dad made it to the car. Her dad helped her up.

"Have a good day, sweetie," he hugged her. "We're talking about this later."

Mrs. Fairchild hugged her as she got in the front seat.

"Oh, honey, I'm sorry about everything," she started rambling. "If only we knew what was going on, we could have prevented all of this from ever happening."

"It's okay, Mom," Cass said. "I kinda realized something last night."

"What is it?" her mom looked her in the eyes and turned the radio down.

"Betty Green didn't kill Mr. Benson, it was Mrs. Jep—" she got cut off by her mother.

"Cass, enough with the murder talk! What's really plaguing you with anxiety? Is it too much homework? Track and field? Your siblings? Is it boys?"

Cass facepalmed.

"Mom, the police have the wrong person in jail! I helped them put an innocent woman in there! We need to fix it! I realized that at the restaurant last night! Mrs. Jepsen was having an affair and killed him! She probably tried to plant evidence on Mrs. Green and I was too stupid to take the bait."

"You're not stupid, honey," her mom said. "Never talk about yourself like that. You're just stressed and need to rest."

"Mom! I got plenty of sleep last night," Cass lied. "I need to contact the police and also Lenore. I think she realized this all last night, too."

Cass' heart began to race, and she knew the heart monitor was going to go off any second. If her mom heard the machine's sounds, she'd stop her from seeing Lenore. She took a deep breath and started thinking of countrysides, beaches, and other picturesque scenes to slow it down. And it worked.

"Well, you're not doing anything until you at least shower," her mom said, fixed on the road.

"Why?"

"You look like a mess. Before you do anything, get changed. I'll call Mrs. Hurley to drop off Lenore if that will make you relax."

Cass sighed. At least Lenore was coming over. She looked at her smartphone, which was at fifteen percent battery. She could at least charge it while she cleaned herself.

After taking a shower, Cass desperately wanted a nap. But she'd have to avoid the urge if she wanted to get proper justice served. She yawned as she dressed, hoping to find a shirt big enough to cover the heart monitor. The Kevin Scarpino concert t-shirt worked for her as she remembered Mrs. Hurley buying them adult sizes last year.

Cass was still brushing her damp hair when the doorbell rang. She raced downstairs and flung open the front door before her mom could casually stroll to it. Lenore stood there, circles under her eyes and carrying a backpack, herself.

"Hey, nice shirt!" Lenore exclaimed. "Hi, Mrs. Fairchild."

"Hello, Lenore, come in," Cass' mother said. "Can I get you anything?"

"I'm fine, thanks."

Both girls ran upstairs to Cass' bedroom, and she shut her bedroom door. Lenore sat on her bed as Elroy jumped up, ready for cuddling.

"So, how was the hospital?" Lenore asked as she pet the cat mindlessly.

"Well, it turns out I really don't have precog," Cass said. "It's just anxiety, which at this point makes me feel better than thinking everything was going wrong because of my feelings."

"Sorry about misinterpreting that," Lenore said. "I didn't know anxiety did all that stuff."

"Not your problem, but now I have to wear a heart monitor for a week."

"Yikes."

"I know. But I have something bigger to tell you."

"So do I."

"Mrs. Green was framed and the real killer is—"

"Mrs. Jepsen!" Lenore interrupted.

"Yes! Wait, how do you know that?"

"Last night, when you were passed out, I thought about how Mrs. Green wasn't lifting anything at the garden party. She couldn't lift a body. Plus, her having the stroke doesn't mean it was the same year Mr. Benson asked for money. But Mrs. Jepsen was free on Sundays and so was Mr. Benson. How did you figure it out?"

Cass explained to her the awkward bathroom conversation she had with Mrs. Jepsen the night before. Lenore gasped at the end of it all.

"Also, I forgot to mention, Mrs. Jepsen said some weird things to me, like how you were 'chasing feelings.' Isn't that weird?" Lenore asked.

"Yeah, she said some weird things to me, too," Cass thought about it. "She told me you weren't invested in the case because of Kevin Scarpino—"

Lenore gasped. "She used him against me?!"

"And she convinced me to bring the rubies to the open house and then never gave them back," Cass said. She paused for a moment in shock. "Oh my gosh, how am I so stupid! I literally gave her evidence to pin it on Betty Green!"

"She made us yell at each other and do extra push-ups at school!" Lenore got angry.

"She really did try to break us up, that heifer!" Cass said. "Well, she's going to learn that you don't go up against us and win."

"Yeah!" Lenore high-fived her best friend. "So, what now?"

"Well, I think I still have the detective's phone number."

"Ugh, that guy?" Lenore rolled her eyes.

"He's a lot nicer than you think." Cass said.

Detective Gomez was typing up his report on a bicycle theft at his desk. He couldn't wait to end his shift and go home and watch some college football. Anything to break up the monotony of the day. He had accidentally put his phone on silent earlier in the day to not get distracted, but his work phone sat there, blank as a whiteboard during the summer.

He leaned back in his chair and kept thinking about the Benson case. Mrs. Green cried the whole time he interviewed her. He didn't even try to push her, but she just said she was guilty and not to punish her hard. She signed the confession form and even nodded when he showed her the evidential love letters found under her bed. She said she didn't know how it got there but then claimed it.

Mrs. Green was out on bail, but Gomez really hoped they could get a psychologist to talk to her. She was probably withholding something. He frowned as he thought of the case even after Sergeant Fuller congratulated him. Something didn't sit right.

His work cell phone started vibrating, and Gomez almost fell out of his chair. He picked up the phone and smirked when he saw the caller ID.

✳✳✳

Mrs. Fairchild was surprised when the doorbell rang again. She was even more surprised when the tall and dark-haired detective was on her porch.

"Can I help you, sir?" she asked.

"Yes, I am Detective David Gomez with Moon Town PD. Your daughter called me about Mr. Benson's murder."

Mrs. Fairchild was confused. Mrs. Hurley's face turned red. She didn't know whether to ground her daughter and her friend or let her go at this point.

"Cassandra Felicity! You have a guest!" she yelled.

She tried her best to put on a happy face for the detective.

Cass and Lenore hurried down the stairs. Cass held her tote bag at the ready.

"Detective," Cass greeted him as she avoided eye contact with her mom.

"Miss Cass," he said. "Miss Hurley."

"Hi," Lenore offered.

"We got the wrong murderer!" Cass started. "Betty Green was having an affair—probably—but Mrs. Jepsen killed Mr. Benson!"

Cass then rapidly updated the detective about everything that happened up to the restaurant.

"That adds up," he said as he scribbled in his notebook. "I'll go visit the Jepsen home."

"Not without us," Lenore insisted.

"What?"

"We're going with you! We helped solve the case while you were probably sitting on your butt bored this morning, hoping to catch the Pitt game in time," Lenore sassed him.

"You're not police, you can't go," he insisted.

"But the Jepsens know us and would be friendlier to you if we came along," Cass inserted herself. "They might not deny you if we were there for some nice innocent reason."

"Well, it depends what your mothers thinks, I guess," Detective Gomez passed off to Mrs. Fairchild.

Mrs. Fairchild shrugged and looked at Mrs. Hurley who was still red in the face.

"You know what, just go solve the case," she said. "If this woman isn't the murderer, you're not investigating this ever again."

Detective Gomez' mouth dropped. This was a new way to discard annoying children.

"So, um, do you have a normal car or an official police car?" Lenore asked as she opened the front door of the house.

Chapter Thirty-Eight

For a government vehicle, it was pretty uncomfortable. Lenore was wriggling in the back seat of Detective Gomez' car. Of course he would let Cass sit up front. At least it was clean.

Lenore sat quietly until she noticed the detective going ten over the speed limit.

"You're speeding," she said as she leaned forward.

"I'm a police officer on a quest," the detective said. "I can speed a little."

"Whatever you say."

He kept driving in silence, still about ten minutes away from the Jepsen home. Everyone was quiet.

"So, do you like police and detective shows?" Lenore asked from the backseat of his car.

"Your dad's an attorney, Miss Hurley," he replied. "Does he like lawyer movies?"

"No, he said they're unrealistic."

"Exactly."

They drove on to the Jepsen home in silence.

"So, you know our guidance counselor, Miss Barber?" Lenore started again. "She totally likes you."

Detective Gomez kept his eyes on the road.

"I'm pretty sure she's single. You could give her your number when this is done."

"Miss Hurley, you've heard the old saying, 'Silence is golden,' right?" he finally spoke up.

"Okay."

More awkward silence. Finally, they were on the Jepsen's street.

"So, um, what do we say when we get there?" Cass asked.

"I'll talk, you two just stay behind me and be quiet," he said.

They pulled up silently to the Jepsen home.

"Heads down, don't look so eager," Gomez warned the girls as they stood behind him.

He knocked plainly on the door, avoiding the chimp door knocker. After a few seconds, John cracked the door a smidge.

"Well, Detective. And girls. Can I help you?" he asked.

"Yes, may we come in?" the detective said, looking through the door.

"Certainly. Sherri has put the child down to nap, but she'll be down," he said.

Cass was back to walking through the familiar entrance. Although, this time it felt much creepier walking through the darkened rooms as her footsteps made the floorboards squeak. *How much were the Jepsens hiding?*

Cass' thoughts were interrupted by Mr. Jepsen shoving a glass of water to her face.

"Here you go," he said as he sat down. "So, what brings you three here today?"

Detective Gomez sat in the tall chair as the girls were back in the loveseat.

"Sir, what were you really doing on the night of Mr. Benson's murder?"

"Pardon?"

"We have some evidence your wife may have assisted in the murder of Edward Benson. Where were you the night of the murder?"

"I was home—that's a fact!"

"And where was Mrs. Jepsen?"

"Also home with me!"

Detective Gomez sighed. He was about to break an old man's heart.

"Mr. Jepsen, do you know where your wife was when you were gone on Sundays?"

"At home, obviously," the old man huffed.

"Did you know she had a weekly visitor when you were gone? A certain gentleman caller?"

"A what?"

"Did you know your wife was cheating on you for the last two years with Mr. Benson?" Lenore interjected. Detective Gomez shot her daggers. "Well, it's true. We have the letters, we have the expensive jewelry she wears, we even know she also called Mr. Benson's cats 'the boys,' just like he did."

"But she wouldn't cheat on me!" he said in disbelief. "We were always faithful! Why would she then stab him in the kitchen if she was seeing him?!"

Cass and Lenore gasped. Everyone was silent for a few seconds.

Detective Gomez opened his mouth slightly.

"So, you were home when she stabbed the man, correct?"

"I just walked in and he was on the floor with a knife next to him!" John panicked. "She said he was trying to harm her! We were both scared. We didn't know what to do or who would believe us! My wife would never hurt a flower! She's too gentle! She also wouldn't cheat!"

"Sir, take a deep breath," the detective continued. "What happened after you saw her with the body?"

"Well we washed the knife," he said. "We were too scared to call the police, so we left his body in the woods hoping no one would find him! But look how that turned out!"

Cass and Lenore gasped.

"By Jove," Lenore let out, semi-ironically.

Detective Gomez shot her another look.

"But why would your wife stab Mr. Benson? What was your relationship with him?"

"I don't know," John cried. "She never said she was interested in him! She seemed disinterested in me for a while so I guess I shouldn't be surprised, but I still can't believe it! She said he was threatening her!"

Right then, everyone heard the kitchen back door open.

"Mrs. Jepsen?" Cass called.

There was no response, only the sound of someone running out. The detective and two girls all looked at each other.

"Well, someone go!" Lenore yelled.

Cass bolted out the back door to look for Mrs. Jepsen. Detective Gomez made some calls on his radio and then ran behind her. The barren rose bushes seemed taller to her today. Cass was careful to not get scratched as she saw Mrs. Jepsen running away. She picked up her speed to chase down the old woman, who wasn't stopping at her calls. Her heart started beating faster and faster.

Of course her heart monitor would start beeping at a time like this. At some point, she was five feet away from the woman, surrounded by bare trees, when she heard herself yell.

"Mrs. Jepsen, STOP!"

The old woman turned around, holding up a large knife.

"What are you going to do? Try to trap me with your police wires going off?" Mrs. Jepsen cried.

Cass pulled up her shirt to her belly button to show her heart monitor. She then let her shirt back down and raised both of her hands.

"It's a heart monitor," she said. "It's not a wire. You're okay. It's okay."

"You don't understand!"

"You're right! I don't! I may have never had the love you had, but I care so much about people it hurts sometimes!"

"I loved him so much! I didn't want to kill him! I just got overwhelmed and something came over me! This knife I used keeps haunting me!"

"It's okay, just put the knife down and we can talk."

Mrs. Jepsen still held onto the same knife she'd used to kill Mr. Benson. She'd kept it hidden in the house since she couldn't bear to cut with it again. She kept thinking about it and about what happened. How could she do that to her love?

Cass took a deep breath as the woman lowered the knife, but her knuckles were white around the handle.

"Why did any of this happen?" Mrs. Jepsen began crying.

"What?"

"I just wanted a peaceful life with him! I was going to run away with him and the boys and be happy. We were going to drive away after my grandkids married and the house was paid off. I wish…" she started blubbering, "But of course… Of course, all his special possessions were gone when I tried to go back to his home... It makes it all worse."

"Like his pictures?"

"Not just my pictures! My letters! My cigarettes! My jewelry he bought to cheer me up!"

"Yeah, I wish I hadn't read some of those letters, either!"

"YOU READ THEM?!"

"Well, you were really in love," Cass offered.

Mrs. Jepsen stopped. "Yeah, I really was."

"But why make Mrs. Green take the blame?"

"Oh, old Betty was an easy target, pah!"

"But if the letters you left were yours, why was she claiming them?"

"How do you know about those?"

"You placed it there after she left the bedroom the day of the garden party," Cass said.

"Wait, you know about that?"

"So, were you both having affairs?"

"Yes."

"Oh, then what's the deal with the big mess she made about the same time as the murder?"

"Her lover happened to be there when her husband came home. They passed it off as something else, but Joe might know something. So she was worried."

"But why did she confess to the murder then?"

"Because I threatened to tell Joe about her affair if she didn't. I visited her in jail and told her. She doesn't know what I know."

"That's…" Cass was at a loss for words. Who on earth were Lenore's neighbors? "… pretty dark."

Mrs. Jepsen shrugged as she held onto the knife. Cass stood her ground, but she was still worried. Her heart monitor continually went off. She really wished she hadn't run out to be faced down by a crazy lady with a knife.

"Put down the knife, Mrs. Jepsen. It's okay," Cass said.

"It's not okay! It's never going to be okay! I need to see him again!" she pointed the knife to herself.

"It's okay, Mrs. Jepsen! You really cared for someone. You cared for someone so much you dug yourself in a hole! You don't need to go through with this!"

"What would you know about that? You've never loved!"

"Hey!" Cass took a little offense. Maybe Mrs. Jepsen was right. Better to let your ego bruise for a bit, though, than have her use that knife.

"You're right! The most I've gotten to love is this cute guy at my school, but we're not dating or anything. But I understand you! I used to think I needed to go investigating things based on my feelings because something bad was happening. I went so hard trying to investigate this case. I just ended up in the hospital after blacking out! It's hard sometimes to not push yourself! But you're actually fine! There's plenty to live for."

"Is there?" Mrs. Jepsen said.

"Of course! Just because you aren't with anyone doesn't mean you can't be happy! There's no need for violence."

Mrs. Jepsen hesitated. Cass tried to back away without her

noticing when she heard the footsteps of others behind her.

"Put the knife down! Mrs. Jepsen, you're under arrest for the murder of Edward Benson! Put your hands up!" Detective Gomez yelled from behind Cass.

Mrs. Jepsen's frail hands shook as she dropped the knife. Cass jumped back a little as it fell into the ground. Detective Gomez hurried over and handcuffed the old woman. She teared up as uniformed officers ran around and secured the scene.

CHAPTER THIRTY-NINE

"Well, I guess I already used my one call," Lenore winked at Cass.

"Lenore, you're so tacky," Cass laughed.

The two were sitting in the police department lobby, waiting for their parents to pick them up.

After Detective Gomez handcuffed the Jepsens, the police took them to the sheriff's office while the girls rode back with the detective.

"WE DID IT!!" Lenore cheered as Cass squealed. Detective Gomez grimaced at the high pitches.

"I KNOW!" Cass shouted.

"I can't believe it! Can you?"

"No!"

They were high-fiving between the console.

Detective Gomez cleared his throat.

"Girls, I can't hear the scanner if you're shouting," he said icily. "Can you keep it down, and let your parents know I'm dropping you off at the station?"

Cass pulled out her phone and opened her notes app for the two of them to message back and forth. They started giggling after a few minutes.

"Hey, now that we got the murderess, you can ask out Miss Barber!" Lenore cheered.

"Yeah!" Cass joined in. "She will say yes if you ask her out. You're a hero now!"

"Say it with me, girls. Silence is…" he said.

They stopped teasing and went back to messaging in Cass' notes app. He was out of his misery after pulling into the police department a few minutes later. Detective Gomez told them to wait at the front for their parents as he walked past the front desk to his office.

The receptionist sat behind a half-cement, half-glass wall, keeping her eyes on her monitor. Between the crime prevention posters and the clock ticking, nothing interesting was happening as they sat.

Lenore couldn't take the silence anymore.

"So, you're okay? The heart monitor didn't break from all that stress?" Lenore asked.

"No, I don't think they can," Cass shrugged. "But it's honestly more itchy with all the sticky pads than anything."

"We solved the case and that detective somehow thinks we're the annoying ones," Lenore rolled her eyes.

"Well, at least he actually believed us," Cass said. "I think your mom is going to kill me even though we got it right."

As they waited for one or both of their moms to pick them up, a young woman with a camera walked up to the receptionist behind a glass window.

"Hi, my name is Tara Gleeson, and I'm with WSDG. I heard on the scanner earlier that the police found Edward Benson's actual killer this afternoon," the woman said. "Is there anyone I can talk to today?"

The receptionist looked at the schedule of ranked officers and tried dialing numbers. The reporter was quietly tapping her foot. Lenore got up from her seat and walked up to the reporter confidently.

"Hey, we were actually there at the scene," she said with doe eyes and a sweet voice.

"Sure," the reporter said casually.

"Really," Lenore said. "The murderer pointed a knife at my friend over here."

"And can you actually prove that to me?"

"For one thing, we have the notebook we tracked the case with," Cass said, pulling it out of her tote bag. She jumped up and showed it to her. The journalist looked interested as she flipped through some pages. "We actually were with the police detective who solved the case, David Gomez. If you have his number, he's in right now doing the paperwork."

The reporter smiled at her. She picked up her phone and started a text as the receptionist kept trying to dial numbers.

***

That night, Cass and Lenore stayed up in the Hurley den to watch the news. Both started squealing as the news music started.

"Tonight, the police got a real murderer to confess. How two minors helped them out. Then, is the city raising parking tickets too high? One councilwoman speaks out," the news anchor read.

"So, Tara Gleeson, the real murderer in a cold case was arrested today?" anchor Jack Lemon asked.

The screen cut to the reporter from earlier standing outside the police station.

"That's right, Chad. The Moon Town Police Department arrested a woman who said she set up a neighbor for the murder of Edward Benson a few months ago," Tara began. "Sherri Jepsen, seventy-four, admitted to police that she killed Benson and then blamed the crime on Betty Green, a fellow church member of St. Mark's Episcopal Church. Detective David Gomez said false confessions are possible."

The camera cut to Detective Gomez looking uncomfortable in

front of the police department sign. The camera panned to B-roll of him talking to other on-call police and him fake-working with a blank computer.

"Well, she was crying the whole time she confessed, and something didn't seem right. I'm glad we have the right person now."

"According to police, Sherri Jepsen stabbed Benson and then dragged his body with her husband, John Jepsen, to the woods. The police learned the new information after talking to two minors who were also helping with the case."

Both girls squealed. The shot changed to a talking head of Lenore át the station and switched to B-roll of the girls showing the notebook pages and the woods behind Mr. Benson's house.

"We found Mr. Benson's body in the woods, and we both knew we had to solve the case for him," Lenore said. "We took extensive notes over our interviews with neighbors and anyone else who had information."

The shot changed to B-roll of Cass, as Tara went over how Cass was threatened in the woods after the girls and Gomez went to the residence.

"Yeah, it was scary, but we also got the truth, so that's what matters," Cass' eyes sparkled on TV. "We're happy to do this for Mr. Benson and his family."

"John Jepsen faces charges of lying to police and obstruction. Sherri faces charges of murder, blackmail, verbal menacing with a deadly weapon, lying to police, disposing of evidence, and obstruction of justice. Both are still in county jail and are being held on five-hundred-thousand-dollar bonds.

"From the Moon Town PD, this is Tara Gleeson, WSDG news."

Both girls high-fived.

"Can you believe it! We're TV famous! I thought the newspaper was going to get us first." Lenore smiled.

"There is probably some paper editor crying right now as he just watched that report," Cass smiled.

Right then, a phone rang throughout the house. Lenore let one of her parents get it at the second ring. After a few minutes, both girls sat still as Mr. Hurley descended down the stairs.

"Hey girls, we're excited to see you on the TV, but we just got a call from one of the other news channels asking to interview you both. It's after eleven," he said. "Next time solve a case for the six o'clock news, please. Also, we may have to use you both as witnesses for when this case goes to court."

"Okay," Cass said.

"Okay, Dad, good night," Lenore said as her dad turned around.

The girls continued watching the news waiting for the story about New Yorkers waiting in line to smell a stinky plant. Lenore sighed when the news also announced indie rock singer Kevin Scarpino posted that he bought a house outside of Pittsburgh in a gated community.

"He just didn't want you to be his neighbor," Cass joked. "Or get murdered."

"Hey, you wore his shirt today!" Lenore said.

"Only to cover my heart monitor," Cass admitted. "It's baggy shirts for me all week."

"Fun."

Cass quickly fell asleep that night and was thrown into her dream. She was in the same forest, but the morning light shone through the trees as the grass peaked through the fallen leaves left from the fall. She wasn't bundled up for the snow anymore. She looked down expecting to find Mr. Benson's body but saw a pair of old brown leather shoes.

"My eyes are up here, dear," she heard a raspy voice speak.

She stood face-to-face with Mr. Benson. He looked dead, but there were no longer blood stains on his sweater vest. He smiled.

"Thank you," he said gently.

Cass woke up to the early sunrise peeping through the den's windows. It was six a.m. She took a deep breath and tried to sleep for another hour before church.

✳✳✳

That morning, the girls ate pancakes after church at the Hurley residence as the news vans swarmed around them. Lenore's parents turned down most of the interviews since the house was dirty and they didn't want the attention to go to their daughter's head. It all stopped when the newspaper called in the early afternoon. The reporter working alone that weekend wanted to simply talk over the phone.

"So, were you girls scared at all?" cub reporter Ben Tim asked over speakerphone.

"All the time, but we had to push past it to solve the case," Cass said.

"Yeah, it was pretty intimidating, we searched for clues during an open house," Lenore said. "Granted, I met Kevin Scarpino, but I was scared we'd get caught by the realtor."

"So, tell me about the notebook you guys have. I heard you did extensive research." Tim changed subjects.

"Yeah, we wrote down all the evidence we could find," Lenore said.

"But we mainly used it to write down what the suspects said and what we read off of them," Cass said. "So, when we had the interview with the Jepsens the first time, I noticed Mrs. Jepsen saying nice things about him. I overlooked it at first, but in hindsight, it makes sense."

"Wow, you're both very thorough," Tim said. "Is there anything else you'd like to tell me that I didn't ask?"

"Crime doesn't pay, and the power of friendship solves the mystery again," Lenore said triumphantly.

"Well," Cass said. "I would say this wasn't an easy case to solve, and it took everyone to get to the bottom of it. Between friends, neighbors, and police, we all contributed to solving the case. Also don't overextend yourself or you'll end up hurt."

"Thanks," Tim said. "Make sure to email me those photos of the mystery notebook. We might use it for art. This will be in tomorrow's edition."

"Thanks," Both girls said, then Mrs. Hurley hung up the phone.

"Okay, both of you get your coats, let's get going," she said.

The girls followed Lenore's mom's instructions and got into the minivan with her. Both were silent on the drive through town as Mrs. Hurley's car played soft pop. The afternoon sun shifted to an overcast sky, rendering the girls quiet and keeping to themselves. During the drive, Mrs. Hurley pulled over to The Roast of Moon Town.

"C'mon, get out," Mrs. Hurley said.

"Wait, you're actually treating us?" Lenore asked.

"Yes, but we're getting drinks to go," she said. "There's a difference between solving mysteries about class cheaters and gossips versus solving an actual mystery. Now, we don't have all day, so I'll be waiting here."

Lenore and Cass ordered their extravagant smoothies with their saved allowances. Before finishing the order, Cass got an idea.

"Can we also get one black coffee?" she asked.

"What size?" the barista replied.

"Small," both girls said. Lenore locked eyes with her best friend.

They got back in the car with their drink holder and closed the door.

"I don't need a coffee, girls," Mrs. Hurley said.

"Don't be mad, Mom, but this coffee isn't for you," Lenore responded.

"Why?" she asked

"You'll see," Lenore said.

Both girls sat in silence, drinking their smoothies without much dialogue. Mrs. Hurley almost felt like she was in another dimension with their introspection. After twenty minutes, they arrived at Western Hill Cemetery.

Lenore's mom handed her a bouquet of lilies and wildflowers. They tiptoed through the graves until they found Mr. Benson's, which had more grass slowly peeking through, making it look less fresh.

Lenore placed the new flowers in front of his headstone. Cass said a silent prayer for Mr. Benson's soul as she placed the to-go cup of coffee next to the flowers.

"So, are you girls going to say anything?" Mrs. Hurley asked.

"Mr. Benson, you were a quiet old man who I thought was weird when you were alive," Lenore started. "It turns out you actually had a double life, which was cool. I hope what we did after you were gone makes up for all the speculation I made when you were alive. Also, Merlin is doing well, but whenever I say 'food' he starts hounding me. Why did you have to spoil him? That's my only complaint. I hope you're resting in peace."

"Mr. Benson, I'm sorry I didn't get to know you when you were alive," Cass said. "Maybe we could have helped you, at least with the loneliness. The past few months have been so crazy, I almost thought I wouldn't survive. Thank you for telling me to keep going in my dreams. Also, Elroy also gets hyper when my mom opens cans. But otherwise he's a great cat. Enjoy that coffee before it goes cold."

Mrs. Hurley made the girls say another prayer and led them back to the minivan.

"WAIT!" Lenore yelled as they walked back to the car. She dashed back to the grave as Cass followed her.

"What's wrong?" Cass asked.

"I almost forgot," Lenore said as she reached into her purse. She pulled out the framed photo of a professional shot of Mr. Benson with his cats. She set it in front of the headstone.

"Okay, now rest in peace," she said.

"Seriously?" Mrs. Hurley asked from behind the girls. "You took the photo?"

"Well, if it was important enough for him to frame, I figured it was important to keep around, Mom," she said. "But don't worry, I made some photocopies at school a few weeks ago to keep in the mystery notebook and my scrapbook."

Mrs. Hurley sighed as she led the girls back to the car. They were good, odd kids.

✲✲✲

That Monday, Cass and Lenore were bombarded by classmates who'd seen them in the news that weekend. Their female classmates crowded them in the locker room.

"You guys solved a murder case this weekend?!" Erin Lee exclaimed.

"Yeah," Cass said casually.

"I thought you guys weren't friends anymore," Emma Stanwell said.

"We worked things out," Lenore said as she stepped onto a bench. "Any more questions?"

All of their classmates were suddenly talking over each other, asking what happened that weekend. Cass and Lenore edited their answer, telling people they had met up at Beijing Gardens, and realized Mrs. Jepsen was the murderer after dinner. They left out the panic attack and Cass waking up in a hospital. Lenore said they talked to police the next day and helped get her in the woods.

"So, did the murderer try to hurt you?" Anna Andrews asked.

"No," Cass said. "I mean, she pointed the murder weapon at me, but I wasn't going to die. The police were right behind me."

"That's so cool," Jada said. "You stood up to a murderer."

"So, you guys really are amateur detectives," Becky Walker said.

None of them realized they missed the first period bell and

the Pledge of Allegiance. Coach Webber walked in expecting another fight.

"Okay, who's fighting now?" he yelled.

Everyone stared at him.

"I don't know what's going on here, but class has started. Get out in the next ten seconds or everyone is running the mile!" he yelled. The locker room was finally empty. He turned to Lenore and Cass.

"What happened now?" he asked.

"Oh no, we're friends now," Cass said.

"But why was every girl in here looking at you?"

"Did you not see the news this weekend, sir?" Lenore asked.

"I don't have cable," he said.

"Well, we solved that murder case and got the real killer," Cass said.

"Good for you," Webber said. "Now get out of the locker room and run laps with everyone else, Hurley. Fairchild, bleachers."

Honored as Cass was by her classmates, she really wanted to avoid people so they wouldn't notice the heart monitor. She and her mom searched all of her drawers the night before to find baggy shirts to conceal it for the week. She thankfully got a note from the doctor to sit out of PE class. Her classmates enviously stared at her as she sat in the bleachers reading as they did laps.

She got through most of the day and was fine by lunch.

"So, have you read your story in the newspaper?" Jada asked. She looked for lunch monitors before handing her phone to the two girls.

The story headline was at the top of the screen and read, "Correct suspect arrested: woman in custody after admitting to cold case murder." The photo that accompanied it was Mrs. Jepsen's mugshot. She looked angry, but her eyes seemed to let out a deep sadness. Lenore skimmed the article.

"We're not mentioned until the eleventh paragraph, but hey, they spelled my name right!"

"Two twelve-year-olds, Lenore Hurley and Cass Fairchild, also assisted the case. According to Gomez, they helped give him the information needed to put away Jepsen.
'They were very useful, and we could not have done it without them,' Gomez said."

"Aw he really appreciates us, that Detective Gomez," Lenore interrupted the article.

"Since when did you start liking Detective Gomez?" Cass asked.

"He's finally giving credit where credit is due," Lenore said. "I appreciate it."

"Get back to reading it, Lenore!"

"Okay,

"Both girls said they kept a notebook where they wrote down the clues and detailed every interview with the suspects.
'Mr. Benson is my neighbor, so we had to do this for him,' Hurley said.
'We couldn't let this case go even if we hit a wall in the investigation,' Fairchild said.'"

Lenore read their quotes excitedly. "Hey look, they added our picture of the mystery notebook at the bottom of the article!"

"My uncle used to work in newspapers," Katie announced. "He said they only ran pictures online when they didn't have enough content."

"Well, at least we still got some coverage," Cass said. She and Lenore continued to read the article even though they were no longer mentioned after two more paragraphs.

Cass perked up for the rest of the day, even as she walked into math class. Nothing could bring her down.

That was until Mrs. Leary sprung a sudden vocabulary pop quiz on the students during her English class. Cass sat there trying to remember all the recent definitions when her heart monitor suddenly went off.

Jacob Louis in the front of the class perked his head up from his desk.

"What is that? Is an alarm going off?" he asked.

Other kids' heads perked up asking if it was a tornado siren from the county or a new school bell.

"I'm not sure," Mrs. Leary said as she looked around.

"It's probably nothing," Lenore said, making dagger eyes at Jacob. He turned back to his quiz.

"Alright everyone, settle down and I'll try to figure it out," Mrs. Leary said.

Cass tried to sigh silently at the sound of the monitor. She waited for the other kids to put their heads back down to approach Mrs. Leary. She was grading the previous classes' quizzes.

"Um, hey Mrs. Leary," she whispered. "That sound is my heart monitor."

Mrs. Leary gave a look of surprise.

"Oh, I'm so sorry Miss Fairchild," she whispered back.

As soon as Cass sat back down, Mrs. Leary told everyone not to worry about the noise.

"Anyone still looking around needs to get back to their quiz," Mrs. Leary announced.

Cass felt self-conscious, as if everyone was staring at her now. But why should she care?

She took down a murderer while wearing it. Mrs. Jepsen knew of it, but she had bigger problems to worry about at the moment. It's not like she'd gossip about the thing attached to Cass' chest to her cellmate or something.

While she felt like she'd conquered a giant, there were still the trolls she worried about. Lenore had her back, but it wasn't going to make middle school any less torturous. After everything she went through, she didn't want to have to fend for herself at the moment.

Cass told herself to pull it together and finished the pop quiz around the same time as her classmates. Mrs. Leary moved on to the grammar lesson for the day. Everyone else was settled by then.

After school, Cass was walking to her locker when she took the wrong turn and ended up in the eighth grade corridor. It would take longer to get to her locker, but at least that meant her area wouldn't be as crowded when she got there. She walked in between the upperclassmen, hoping to get through before tripping on their backpacks, when she felt a hand poke her back.

"Hey, Cass," Leo said.

"Hey!" Cass said as she felt herself blush.

Oh no, please don't go off, heart monitor, she thought.

"So, are you feeling better? I saw you and Lenore solved the case."

"Yeah, I don't really know how to explain what happened Friday night," Cass scratched her head. "But when I went to the bathroom, I ran into Mrs. Jepsen and realized she'd framed Mrs. Green. But I'm okay now. I'm good. Nothing to worry about. How are you?"

"Oh, I'm good. Just another Monday. I was surprised when my family watched the news this weekend and we saw you and Lenore there," he redirected the conversation. "That's so cool! But what now for you both?"

"Probably just homework after school and get prepared for track and field season."

"Oh okay," Leo said. "Some of my friends say I should pick up a different sport this year since the old baseball coach quit and they're still looking for a replacement. Also, it might help when I go to high school next year and have some more friends."

"Yeah, that would be nice," Cass said as her heart raced.

"I don't know whether to do baseball or track and field. Does track and field cut people after tryouts?"

"You get in as long as you have a pulse," Cass said.

"Okay, well then I guess I'll see you on the track come March," he smiled.

"Okay, see you," Cass walked away.

She sighed, feeling like an idiot after that conversation. As she walked by some now-empty classrooms, her heart monitor stopped beeping. Did she get through a whole conversation with Leo while this went off? The eighth graders must have been so loud they drowned out the technology strapped to her chest.

She passed by the front office where she saw Miss Barber standing next to the receptionist. She was smiling into her phone as she was typing. Cass wasn't sure who she was texting, but she'd bring this up to Lenore later.

While waiting for their parents to pick them up outside, Lenore read the newspaper she picked up from the school library. She was perusing the inside pages as Cass looked for her mom's car.

"Hey, look here, Cass!" Lenore exclaimed. "In police reports, there's a report of a break-in at the fourteen hundred block of York Court! Isn't that where Marnie lives? It says someone broke a window, entered, and stole some jewels and a beloved miniature schnauzer."

"Marnie doesn't have a schnauzer, though," Cass said. "Wait, you're not thinking of investigating, are you?"

"What's the harm?"

"Well, my heart monitor isn't going off, so there's a sign for you," Cass smirked.

"Okay, okay, I'll take a break from cases," Lenore said.

"Good."

"But only for a week."

"Lenore."

"A month?"

"No."

"Six months?"

"Yeah, that probably works for me."

Epilogue

Cass was more than relieved to finally get the heart monitor taken off at the end of the week. The doctors looked at her and told her parents technobabble as she sat there. Both her mom and dad kept smiling at her like nothing was wrong. Cass never wanted to wear that thing again.

The next step was weekly counseling. Every Tuesday, she now skipped winter conditioning to go see Dr. Bianca Gates in her white office, which had vague modern art and an old couch. Dr. Gates seemed surprised that Cass was open about everything she asked. In reality, Cass wanted to get better, so she let loose everything she was thinking and whatever troubled her. She appreciated Dr. Gates teaching her new techniques to help with the anxiety.

Three weeks after Mrs. Jepsen's arrest, Cass was sitting in pre-algebra taking another test. The first few questions weren't too difficult, but she felt herself stumbling through the fifth question. That's when the menacing thoughts came to her.

You can't do this. You're doomed. Give up now. You'll fail. They're coming for you, they're coming for you. It's over now. It's over, it's over, It's over. It's so over.

Cass looked at her paper and sighed. She then told herself to stop looking at her paper. Okay, first sense is sight. She locked in on Lenore sitting a few rows ahead of her, filling out the sheet nonchalantly. The second sense is hearing. She listened to her classmates writing their answers. The tapping of pencils was almost calming. Third sense, smell. Oh, gross, she forgot she was next to Connor Flemming, who just got out of gym class. Fourth, taste. How would she do that? Lick her paper? Cass felt the spittle in mouth and decided that qualified. Fifth, touch. She made sure to wear her comfiest sweater to class. No itch at all. She was glad she picked it for a day like this.

She thought about all her senses again and then looked back at her paper. Suddenly question five wasn't as difficult anymore. Cass smiled as she took on the problem.

The End

Acknowledgments

My anxiety book is here! I have wanted to publish Cass' story for years. Maybe because it's a little bit based on my own story of anxiety (minus the precognition and murder). Maybe because I hope this book will help those Cass' age with anxiety.

There are so many people I want to thank for all the support for this project. Thank you to my gorgeous husband Justin for his unrelenting support. I wrote this for Nanowrimo 2020 and he would sit in my living room while I wrote on weekends.

Thank you to my fabulous editor Sarah Waterman. Thank you for pulling out the ideas from my head and helping me put them on paper. And for the edits. And all the help with my blurb. And all my endless follow up questions.

Thank you to Julia Horobets for another beautiful cover. You are the best.

Thank you Sage, Pattie, Allison, Ollie, and Jennifer.

Thank you reader, for making it this far and taking your time to read this story dear to my heart. I hope you liked it.

Gaby Knight is a former journalist and a current anxious detective existentialist. She lives in Alabama with her husband, Justin, cats, Luna and Cleo, and dog, Lassie. You can follow her on Instagram at GabyKnightAuthor.